PROMISED LAND

Borgo Press Fiction by BRIAN STABLEFORD

PROMISED LAND

HOODED SWAN, BOOK THREE

BRIAN STABLEFORD

THE BORGO PRESS

MMXI

PROMISED LAND

DEDICATION

By special request, this book is dedicated to everybody in the world except "Viv"

CONTENTS

CHAPTER ONE

NEW ALEXANDRIA IS NOT THE ideal world for an uncultured slob to be stranded on. It's not so much that its population consists almost entirely of bespectacled bibliophiles who are deeply into the philosophy of civilisation and temperance, but rather the fact that those inhabitants who do not fit into this category feel somehow ashamed of the fact. Everybody on New Alexandria apologises too much. Everywhere you go you can find intellectual lightweights soldiering on under a burden of ersatz education and carefully fashionable good taste.

Personally, I wouldn't mind it so much if they were all getting a big kick out of it, but the glumness which lies just beneath the hypocrisy really puts my back up. Every time I went out to have a drink in Corinth I got edgy. I usually had to take Nick or Johnny along with me in case my sorrows ended up drowning me instead of vice versa.

I had a lot of spare time to fill in on New Alexandria after the Rhapsody business, and Corinth was the nerve centre of Charlot's theatre of operations. Charlot had a lot of work to catch up on following the Rhapsody catastrophe. I think his pride had been a little bit hurt by the outcome of that affair—not a single one of the famed wonder-worms had survived the rigours of contact with humanity, and yet another agent of destruction was temporarily lost to galactic society. Ripped off from their cosy little cave, the worms had shown a healthy interest for a matter of days, and then decided the whole thing wasn't worth it, curled up their metaphorical toes and retired gracefully into protoplasmic goo. Who could blame them? Not me, that's for sure. I was secretly gleeful. Secretly, because it would have been less than diplomatic to gloat while Charlot was in a bad mood.

In any case, my name was mud. Charlot had elected to believe that at least some part of the blame for the whole mess was mine. The sad fate of his prize specimens had soured any sympathy which might have lingered on from the moment when we had stood together facing the wrong end of Bayon Alpart's powergun. Charlot's answer to the bad mood, apparently, was to throw himself wholeheartedly into his work and forget all about his wonderful little toy, the *Hooded Swan*. I was left kicking my heels, but Nick and Eve had other jobs to do back on Earth, where the number two supership (the *Sister Swan*) was having her teething troubles. They took Johnny back with them a couple of times, as consultant engineer, but because this baby really was going to be Eve's ship, they had no use for me. I wished her well of her new opportunity. It can't have been much fun for her to have lost her first ship to me at the last moment—especially such a ship as the *Hooded Swan*, and to such a cynical reprobate as myself. I wasn't much interested in the sister ship, anyhow. My attachment to the *Hooded Swan* was personal, and I couldn't help but think of the *Sister Swan* as a rival.

There was nothing for me to do but bum around in Corinth, alone or with whoever was available. I didn't get particularly bored. Every minute of the two years which I owed Charlot that didn't involve me putting my neck into some version of the lion's mouth was profit as far as I was concerned. I was perfectly content to kick my heels forever—until freedom day, anyway. My debt to the Caradoc Company was being discharged at about thirty a day, which was damn good money for no work.

I knew it couldn't last, of course. Charlot would inevitably get around to thinking up some small favour I could do him, and it would probably have a nasty touch to it, just to pay me back for the imagined wrongs I'd perpetrated on Rhapsody and in the Halcyon Drift. Every day I expected to be presented with some crazy commission for hunting up irrelevant information in some hellhole, or asked to go and break some record.

The waiting got to Johnny, while he was actually around. So much so that he wasn't really very good company. I lived in hope that months of constant association with yours truly must inevitably result in some kind of intellectual contamination, and that he might gradually get less eager and more sane. But no results were showing up as yet. The kid had an imaginary bomb up his backside and he couldn't sit still without suffering all kinds of psychosomatic disorders. This led me to seek company elsewhere, and I developed an acquaintance with a policeman named Denton who never seemed to have any work to do. He was one of these guys with a penchant for hanging around, easy to talk to and at least part of the way to being a thoroughly good bloke. My checkered past hadn't really been conducive to my forming beautiful relationships with the representatives of the law, but at this point in time I had a crystal-clear conscience, and fraternisation seemed almost natural.

Once or twice, though, I couldn't help feeling the urge to get clean away from the whole Corinth scene. I wasn't restless, just a little claustrophobic. One bad day while Nick was on Earth and Eve was somewhere else entirely, Johnny started talking about gambling. I tried to explain to him that nobody but an idiot would play cards with New Alexandrians, but he couldn't grasp my point. It isn't that they cheat, of course, but they have a keen sense of probability and they don't know how to play anything badly. Gambling is an exercise in separating fools from their money, and the only fool abroad in Corinth just then was Johnny Socoro himself. But he couldn't accept that. He kept talking about luck, and if there's one thing I can't stand it's some ingénue giving me lectures on runs of luck and the inadequacies of logic.

I borrowed one of Charlot's fleet of staff cars and lit out for the hills. Theoretically, I was supposed to check with Charlot before leaving the neighbourhood, but of course I didn't bother. By similar theory, I didn't have any right to appropriate the car.

But I've never been a devout believer in sticking too close to the approved mode of behaviour. People don't expect it of me—everybody knows that I'm thoroughly bloody-minded. I have a reputation to keep up.

It was late spring, and the weather was just turning beautiful. I'm no romantic but I can appreciate the look of greenery and the delicacy of flowers, especially after I've been given a hard time. And I had. For two years and more.

The car was a Lamoine 77 and rode with just a hint of vibe even when she was cruising. I like a car which lets me know I'm travelling—who wants to labour under the delusion that he's sitting in a baby carriage? I pushed her along at one-forty, which was just beyond her most comfortable speed. I like to push. And what the hell—it wasn't my car.

I liked the country, and I figured after a couple of hours that I'd like it a lot more if I forgot about the road. Roads are boring. I cut to eighty and moved her out into the open, and then amused myself bouncing bushes and hurdling hills for a while. It felt really good to bowl along, with the wheel in my left hand and the gearshift in my right. I was deliberately rough with the stick. I guess I was joyriding like a kid, but it beat drift-diving and warren-crawling as a way of spending time. You can stand a little self-indulgence occasionally, I figure. Also, I was staying sober and getting a clean, fresh kind of high out of the wind and the sun and the smell.

There were miles and miles of open parkland. Once I'd lost the road it was easy not to find it again. New Alexandria is a garden world—clean cities and tidy, inoffensive countryside. Very carefully planned to look virgin, like a whore with a strong streak of vanity. They'd subjected the hills to artistic cosmetic landscaping. The New Alexandrian character demands that a sticky finger be intruded into every possible pie.

Evening began to creep up, and it felt truly pleasant. I'm not too fond of brightness, and the gentle grey of twilight always turns me on a lot more than the glare of noonday. The airstream grew cold around me, but I didn't put the hood up, or even the screen. It was doing me no harm.

I wasn't really thinking about turning for home—the idea of night driving seemed attractive—when the sky began to darken. In fact, I wasn't really thinking about anything at all. I was at peace with existence, which is somewhere I don't often find myself. I wasn't even trying to remember how long it had been since I'd enjoyed leisure time so much, and I guess my old friend the whispering wind was luxuriating in the feeling as well, because he never said a word.

Then I saw the girl.

She was running, and the moment I saw her I knew that she wasn't inspired by the joys of spring. There was someone after her. I couldn't see them at first, because there was a hill in the way. I put my foot on the brake to slow up while I put my mind back into gear and considered the situation.

There were two men chasing her. They didn't seem to be in anywhere near the hurry she was in. I couldn't read anything into their faces or their manner, but it was a long way in dim light. The idea of rapists on New Alexandria struck me as being pretty incongruous, but I couldn't immediately think of any other reason why a girl should be fleeing two men.

Well, said the wind.

Well what?

Well, do something.

I'm going to, I assured him. No rush. She's got a good fifty yards in hand and they aren't even trying to peg it back. They're letting her run herself into the ground.

All of which was sweetly reasonable. No charging forward for Grainger. This was the kind of thing I'd learned not to rush into. I've never been a great fan of the hero who is always on the lookout for damsels in distress. The idea of knight errantry is wholly repulsive to my pragmatic and ungentlemanly character.

The girl saw me, but she didn't instantly recognise me as a godsend. Rather the reverse, in fact, because she swung aside so that she was running diagonally away from both me and her persecutors. This struck me as being an illogical move. I could overtake her in ten seconds flat and she must have known that. Apparently, she was scared of everybody and suffering from panic. This impression served to reinforce my theory that her pursuers intended her no good.

I eased off the brake and let the Lamoine ooze forward at a fast dawdle. The two men saw me as well. They, apparently, adopted a more rational approach to life. *They* knew that I had the key card. One of them stopped altogether and the other slowed from a jogtrot to an amble and began waving to me. Nobody seemed to think that I was on the side of the angels, despite my hesitancy about rushing in like a fool.

I resolved to give everybody a shock. I swung the car to head for the two men, and stamped on the jerk stud. The Lamoine went four feet up into the air on a quick blast, and shot forward in a long arc at seventy-five climbing toward a hundred. She bounced on air billows all the way, swayed like a haunted drunkard and screamed.

They decided that I wasn't very friendly, and ducked. I missed them both by yards—which was perhaps fortunate as murder is *a priori* evidence of carelessness and a lack of diplomacy—but to hear them howl you'd have thought there were only millimetres to spare.

I U-turned and gentled her back to a smooth flow at the regulation four inches above the grassblades. The girl was looking back over her shoulder, and she didn't seem too reassured by my cavalier treatment of the bogeymen. I realised that she was very scared indeed. She didn't stop running. It never occurred to me then that she might be ten times as scared of me as she was of them, but this was, in fact, not unlikely.

I reined in beside her.

'It's okay!' I yelled—though there was really no need to shout. 'I'm on your side.'

She shied away and I curved through the air after her.

'Save it, kid,' I called. 'Calm down and let's talk it over. Don't worry about *them*.'

She twisted her body to get a good look over her shoulder

at my face. The contortion proved too much for the stability of her headlong flight and she fell over. By the time she was fit to get up, I was out of the Lamoine and beside her. Now she was finally convinced that she was caught, she thought better of bolting again, and allowed herself to collapse back on to the ground, panting fit to burst and beginning to cry.

She was small and thin. She wasn't human but she was very humanoid. I wasn't familiar with her racial characteristics. I had never encountered one of her kind before. Her skin was golden-brown and looked moist. Her eyes were big and orange. Her hands seemed to be very contortive—her fingers were tentacular and retractable. Beneath her clothing there looked to be some kind of ridge pattern on her back. She had no hair.

'It's okay,' I told her, much more gently this time. I wondered whether she spoke any English at all. But I didn't know what other language to try, and I didn't feel like doing a quick run through all the reassuring noises in my repertoire.

The other two were up on their feet again and coming fast. I wondered whether I ought to try and get the girl into the car and flit away into the gathering night, as I was outnumbered. But I decided that she might start an embarrassing struggle, so I elected to wait. Besides which, they were only medium-sized New Alexandrians and I prided myself that as a nasty and brutal outworlder I could probably scare them unconscious if I snarled. I'm not big and hard by any means, but I could put on a convincing act for such as these.

'Well,' I said, as they pulled up a few yards away and looked at me balefully, 'what do *you* want?'

One of them—a black-haired man with pale skin and gold-rimmed spectacles—waved a manicured fingernail at the Lamoine. 'That's one of our cars,' he said, as if expecting an explanation.

'You could have killed us, you crazy bastard,' said the other—a more typical and more commendable reaction, I thought.

'So?' I said, to both of them.

'It's that pilot,' said the second man. He was a typical nonde-script New Alexandrian intellectual second-class citizen. A menial. A hireling. He was pale-brown and small-featured. I didn't know him from Adam, but my notoriety on the planet, and in Corinth particularly, permitted me to be recognised by a great many of the local peasantry.

'My name,' I said to him coldly, 'is Grainger.' I deliberately loaded my voice with loathing.

'We only want to take her back,' said the pale-skinned man.

'Back where?'

'The colony.'

'He doesn't know about the colony,' supplied the other.

'Well *tell* him then,' said the man with the spectacles, 'if he's such a good friend of yours.' He was annoyed.

'I don't know what you must think about this,' began the man who had recognised me, 'but we certainly didn't mean the girl any harm.'

'Well now,' I said, 'what do you reckon?' I addressed myself to the girl. She just crouched there, showing no inclination to rise, but her eyes flickered back and forth from them to me. I couldn't read a thing from her expression. Alien faces are almost always opaque, no matter how human they appear. It takes a long time before you can learn to read them.

'She doesn't speak English,' said the Caucasian.

'My name's Tyler,' said the other, touching the pale man on the arm to bid him be silent while he tried a little tact. 'I work for Titus Charlot.'

'So do I,' I said. 'He doesn't send me out to terrorise little girls.'

'The girl's part of a colony of aliens that Charlot is looking after. She got out tonight and decided to take a run around. She's only a child, she doesn't know any English, and people back at the colony were worried about her. We came out to find her, but she ran away from us. We should have brought a couple of the Anacaona with us, but it didn't occur to us at the time. We don't want to hurt her. We only want to take her home. Do you think that you could give us a lift back to the colony in the car?'

'She doesn't know what she's doing,' murmured the other man.

'This colony,' I said. 'I suppose it's really a research establishment?'

'It's not a bloody concentration camp,' said Tyler. He seemed to be quite offended by the idea. 'These people aren't experimental animals. They're working with Charlot. They're scientists.'

'And you're atomic physicists?' I suggested.

'We're administrative staff. We keep the bloody project going. There are problems, you know, maintaining colonies of offworlders. Or do you always reach for your gun whenever you see an alien? Never met one outside its natural environment before?'

The sneer was so totally unwarranted that I got quite angry about it. The pale man looked a bit disgusted, as he had every right to be after Tyler's unspoken demand to be allowed to handle things.

'Where is this colony?' I snapped.

'Couple of miles back,' said Tyler.

'She gave you a good run, then.'

'Look,' said Tyler, losing his patience visibly. 'There was no harm in the kid taking a walk. But we can't let her wander around out here on her own. We have to look after these people. Lanning and me—we're supposed to see that things run smoothly. Charlot'll have our heads if there's any trouble at the colony, especially if it involves the child. Sure she's scared. But that isn't our fault. We're only doing our job and we haven't time to fool around. Now, we don't want to hurt her, we only want to get her home. If you don't want to give us a lift, fine, but will you please stand out of my way so I can get on with doing what I'm paid to do.'

'Does she want to go with you?' I stalled.

'None of us can ask her, can we?' said the other man—presumably Lanning. 'We don't speak her language.'

'You're in charge of running the colony and you don't speak her language?' I said incredulously.

'They all speak English,' said Tyler. 'Except some of the kids. Hell, man, you know what kids are like. They like to give a bit of trouble. Well, okay, nobody's going to turn her over their knee, unless her daddy does it. But she has to go home. I'm taking her back, and there's not a damn thing you can do about it.'

He stepped forward, and I didn't budge an inch.

Mr Tyler would never have won prizes for diplomacy. Quite the reverse. But he didn't have it in him to force his own way. He was just as tall and heavy and muscular as I was, but he hadn't had the practice. He wasn't a fighter. A bully perhaps, but not a fighter.

'Look,' said Lanning, as Tyler and I stood toe to toe sizing each other up. 'There's no sense to all this. I mean, look at us. We aren't thugs. We aren't rapists.'

I looked at him, as he so kindly invited me to. He was right. He wasn't a thug. It didn't endear him to me, though. They obviously weren't the type any man would hire to do his dirty work for him, so they were probably absolutely on the level. But they'd stirred me up somewhat, and I'm naturally stubborn anyhow.

'You can check with Charlot back at the camp,' said the pale man. 'We've got a call circuit with priority. He'll tell you it's all okay.'

That decided me. I didn't want to be brought on the carpet before Charlot so he could tell me off while Lanning and Tyler had a quiet chortle.

'I don't think I want to give you boys a lift,' I said.

'What about the girl?' said Tyler, in a low voice.

'That's different,' I said. 'I don't mind helping out a lady.'

They couldn't think of anything to say.

'I came out for a pleasure cruise,' I said pensively. 'I guess the young lady must have stepped out to sample the evening air for similar reasons. You morons are spoiling her good time. You can reassure everyone back at the camp that she's in good hands, and I'll have her home within a couple of hours.'

'You can't do that,' said Lanning.

'Watch me,' I said.

He was already taking a caller out of his pocket. He was going to report me to someone at the colony, who would presumably use their priority circuit to alert Charlot. But I was too late changing my mind. I'd already declared my intentions. Perhaps I shouldn't interfere. But I wanted to, and I had.

'Now just you wait a minute,' said Tyler, who had not yet recognised the inevitable.

'Did you speak?' I said pleasantly, looking him in the eyes and smiling. I hope I looked really evil. He backed off a step, pleasing me immensely in the process.

'There's no need for that,' said Lanning. 'You just do what you want to, Mr Grainger. We'll tell everybody concerned that the girl is safe with you. Everything will be fine.'

'That's right,' I said, ignoring his sarcasm. 'Everything will be fine.'

I offered a hand to the girl. She'd calmed down a lot while we three were acting out our little farce. I think she'd gathered that I wasn't in total harmony with her oppressors. She watched Lanning and Tyler turn away. I reached out a hand to her, and she let me help her up. That's a language anyone can understand. I ushered her gently into the front passenger seat of the Lamoine. I took my time moving around into the driver's seat. Tyler was watching me from a few yards away. Lanning was talking rapidly into the caller.

Before I started the car again, I paused and looked around at the deepening night. I drew an appreciative breath and used my face to try and indicate my enjoyment to the girl. Then I smiled.

She smiled back. She was obviously used to the company of humans. She knew what I meant.

After all, I thought, even Titus Charlot smiles.

Sometimes.

CHAPTER TWO

I ROLLED THE LAMOINE around at eighty or ninety for ten minutes or a quarter of an hour while she settled down to the conclusion that everything was pretty much okay.

I tried her with 'What's your name?' and 'Where were you going?' but it was obvious that she didn't know even that much English. I didn't bother to descend to the 'Me Tarzan, who you?' level of attempted communication, and the fancy sign language which works so well in all the soap operas has never appealed to me as a way of getting along. I was quite happy failing to communicate. Nobody needs small talk that badly.

You're a defeatist, accused the wind.

I'm practical, I assured him—not only silently but without moving my lips. I didn't want the young lady to get hold of the idea that I was the kind of filbert who talks to himself.

That has to be a joke, he said, after the way you went barging in and casually picked her up, not knowing who she is or what she was up to.

You know me, I told him. My sympathies are always with the guy who's dodging the gorillas. Damsels, I admit, are not really my line in romantic comedy—not as young as this one, anyhow—but I can always be persuaded to make an exception by some representative of the scum of the earth trying hard to get on my wick.

He *did* know me, of course, and he was getting to the stage where he didn't bother to criticise me too much. I mean, there comes a point when criticism just defeats its own object. I'm impulsive and I'm perverse and I don't mind a bit. And the wind, by virtue of his position, just had to live with it, exactly as I was having to live with him. As time went by, we made a much better job of it. By this time, I think, we were well past the loathing and repulsion *à la* Grainger and the hauteur and intimidation *à la* wind. We were getting to be just good friends. We had reached the stage where I quite appreciated his tired wisecracks and he didn't mean them seriously.

One thing I liked was that he was no kind of a backseat driver. Not in the literal sense, that is. He didn't tell me how to fly, whether I was in deep space or a handspan off the ground. A parasite who can respect his host's professional expertise can't be all bad.

We didn't manage much of a joyride. I was pointing vaguely back toward the suspected direction of the colony, having no real intention of running the kid around till all hours, when I heard a horribly familiar sound. It was the wailing of a siren.

'Hell,' I said pensively, and a little fatalistically. 'The fun's over, folks.'

The girl looked at me strangely with her big orange eyes. Her face looked tragically sad, but that was purely illusion. She might have learned to smile, but she sure as hell hadn't learned to play Hamlet yet. For all I knew, she might be as happy as a skylark.

I made a wry smile, but she didn't return it.

'It's the cops,' I told her, speaking softly and maintaining my rueful grin despite the fact that she didn't seem able to figure it out.

I pulled the Lamoine to a full stop and stepped out. The police were using a flipper, not a car, so it was probably a special consignment, not a regular patrol. I wasn't really worried—not because I imagined that they would understand, but because I was pretty confident that Charlot would bail me out of any trouble short of mass murder.

The cop from the passenger seat dropped to the ground from the hovering flipper and came over. Cops have two styles of

movement. They either swagger with a kind of free-dance interpretation of a Texan drawl, or they stride purposefully like a
second lieutenant with an inflated ego.

This one strode.

He got quite close before I recognised him as my old buddy
Denton.

'Jesus,' I said. 'They even put you to work, hey?'

'Hello, Grainger,' he said. 'You're in trouble. Item: one stolen
car. Item: one abducted girl. Yep, it's all here.'

'I admit it,' I said. 'I am now and always have been in
complete personal control of all organised crime on this world
and two hundred others. What are my chances of bail?'

It wasn't very funny. Sometimes I'm a distinct failure when
it comes to raising a laugh.

'The girl has to go back in the flipper,' said Denton. 'I have
to drive you back to Corinth in the car.'

'Okay,' I said, with more than a hint of sullenness. 'Carry on.
Don't mind me.'

He walked around the car and yanked the far door open. He
gestured to the girl to step out. She didn't move. He took her
gently by the arm, but didn't pull. She got the message, and
stepped into the road. He led her with consummate gentleness
over to the flipper. She looked up at the machine, which was
humming sulkily as it hung suspended in the air. She didn't
want to get up into it, but she was beyond arguing by now.
I think she'd had enough and wanted to go home. I couldn't
blame her. Denton lifted her by the waist and she took his seat
beside the pilot. The pilot strapped her in while his erstwhile
companion sealed the door.

The flipper rose into the sky again.

I waved.

'Goodbye,' I said levelly, keeping an eye on the cop. 'It was
nice meeting you. We must do it again sometime.'

Denton planted himself squarely in front of me and shook his
head tiredly.

'Okay, lover boy,' he said. 'Let's go home and explain to

Daddy.'

'Is Charlot mad?' I asked him. 'Or do you mean the chief of police?'

'I mean Charlot,' he said. 'This is too big for the poor old chief.'

It figured. Nothing moved in Corinth without Charlot's seal of approval. I had a nasty feeling that, old though he was, he could rip a leatherbound copy of the Statutes of New Rome in half with his bare hands.

'I suppose you're going to insist on driving,' I said.

'Orders,' he replied.

'Typical,' I commented. 'It's no way to treat an honest man, you know.'

I was still trying to capture a whimsical mood.

'What's an honest man doing in a stolen car?' he wanted to know.

'Borrowing it,' I told him.

'*I* believe you,' he assured me, 'but it's not my car.'

We took up our assigned positions within the Lamoine and he slid her into gear, taking off with a nasty jerk.

'Clumsy,' I commented. That killed any possible conversation for at least twenty miles.

'Do I take it correctly,' I said finally—to break up the silence—'that I am not actually under arrest: You are, I assume, taking me home solely in the interests of serving the community, as you would assist, say, a lost kitten or a stray alien?'

'I'm just tidying up,' he told me.

'Sweeping the dust under the carpet,' I said humourlessly. 'Who was the girl and why were the two guys chasing her and what the hell would you have done?'

He turned to look at me soberly. 'They *told* you who she was and why they were chasing her,' he said, cop-fashion. Then he added: 'Probably something like you. Only I'd have been a damn sight smarter getting her home. I wouldn't have waited for the trouble to catch up.' That was just because he knew me. I think he'd have given anyone else the usual line—the I-got-a-job-to-do, honest-cop-taking-home-a-steady-wage-to-wife-and-kid line. Cops almost always pretend that they don't know nothing from nothing and they don't much care. I could never be a cop.

I didn't think it was necessary to explain, and I was dead certain that there was no point in protesting. He knew me. We both knew what had happened. I didn't ask him any silly questions about what was going to happen.

Less than half an hour later I was able to ask my questions of the guy with all the answers.

'I don't pay you to act like a crazy kid,' he said, deliberately vulgarising his language to add to the weight of his sneer.

'You don't pay me at all,' I said.

'I pay enough,' he said. 'I'm doing you no disservice by rescuing you from the unfortunate situation in which you found yourself after Caradoc picked you up in the edge of the Drift. I know that you consider that situation quite unjust, but it's the one you have to live with. I know that you don't like me. But you're a reasonable man. Is it too much to ask of you that you cooperate with my men instead of interfering with them just for the hell of it?'

'I'm sorry I borrowed one of your cars without asking,' I said evenly.

'I don't care about the car,' he said, rising snappishly to the bait—which surprised me somewhat. 'I'm talking about the girl.'

'Titus,' I said, in the warmest possible tone, 'if you were riding in your car and saw a very small girl being chased by two not-very-small men who didn't look a bit like sterling citizens, what would you do? Would you really entrust her to their care on their mere say-so?'

'Why didn't you take them all back to the colony?' he said. 'That's what they wanted you to do.'

I considered suggesting that they might have hit me over the head once I turned my back on them, but decided that it was not a wise tack to take. I decided to tell the truth.

'I didn't like them,' I said.

He sighed. 'You're more trouble than you're worth,' he said.

'I couldn't agree more,' I said. 'Shall I pack my bags?'

'No,' he said.

I shrugged. 'Up to you,' I commented.

'Look,' he said. 'You know perfectly well what kind of work I do. I synthesise patterns of thought. I work with a lot of aliens over a long period of time with a large staff. There are half a dozen colonies on New Alexandria. The people live here. They have their homes and their families and their children here. They need a certain amount of looking after. I don't put them in prison camps or on reservations, but they do live together, and to them this is an alien world. The girl was born here, but her parents come from Chao Phrya. She doesn't even speak English, because she isn't concerned with the project. She knows hardly anything about the world except that she's a stranger here. Her education is in the hands of her own people. It was for *them* that Tyler and Lanning went out to fetch her home. Tyler and Lanning are troubleshooters out at the colony. They do lots of odd dirty work. They have a difficult job to do. It isn't made any easier by interference from disinterested parties with some kind of warped quixotic streak. Will you please, in future, leave my staff alone.

'That's all.'

I wanted to tell him to go to hell, but I thought that the time had come for a little graceful retirement. We parted on not the best of terms, but we had never really reached the best of terms. We'd been at war ever since the party at Hallsthammer.

I accepted everything he said, of course. It was none of my business. Why should I even suspect that he was lying? I could have asked to look around his Anacaon colony, but he'd probably have told me to drop dead, and it wouldn't have told me that he had anything to hide.

I have a suspicious mind, but it wasn't always up to coping with Titus Charlot's brand of deviousness.

CHAPTER THREE

AFTER THAT INCIDENT, I decided that irresponsibility was definitely no longer the in thing. I elected to devote myself to more mature and approved pursuits, such as improving my mind and occasionally partaking (always judiciously) of a little intoxicating liquor. I found that my mind could still react favourably to a little improvement. It was more than two years since I'd been able to devote serious time to reading. I'd been too flattened back on Earth before I joined the delArco outfit to do anything except square-eye the HV.

The wind approved thoroughly of my getting deeply into a printed-word bonanza, although his tastes in literature weren't mine by any means. It probably speaks well for my general mood that I compromised instead of having it all my own way. If, that is, you call 80/20 a compromise rather than a concession.

I knew that the peace couldn't last long, but I didn't expect it to be broken in quite the way it was.

I was lying on my bed in the late afternoon when there was an insistent knocking at my door. I couldn't be bothered to get up, so I simply yelled out an invitation to enter.

I didn't expect the Spanish Inquisition.

It was the cops, and there were three of them. That seemed to me to be overdoing things. My old friend Denton was with them (naturally), and he came to talk to me while his buddies stood about flatfooted and looked around suspiciously.

'Where have you been all day?' demanded Denton. I'd already gathered that it wasn't a social call, but he was making sure I retained no illusions. He was still striding instead of walking like normal people, and he talked like a cheesegrater.

'I didn't do it,' I said. 'Whatever it was'

'Never mind the patter,' he whipped back. 'Just answer the questions.'

'Honest,' I said, whimsically stubborn, 'I distinctly remember not doing it and I've got six witnesses who didn't see me.'

'Get up,' he said. 'Let's go'

'To the station?' I inquired. 'Or are we still cutting out the middleman?'

'Charlot,' he said, succinctly.

'Poor old desk sergeant,' I commented. 'Never gets in on any of the fun.'

Denton took the book out of my hand as I eased myself off the bed. He closed it without glancing at it and threw it on to the pillow.

'You lost my place,' I said.

'This isn't funny,' he said. 'This time it's real trouble.'

'What's up?' I wanted to know.

'You answer my questions first.'

'I've been here all day. Also most of the week, except a couple of evenings I've been down the street to the bar and the store, for most of which time my alibi is you. I've got no witnesses for this afternoon, but people see me all the time when I'm outside and at most mealtimes. I haven't touched any of the cars and I haven't committed any other crimes except kicking slot machines and being rude to robots. Now who killed whom?''

'Have you see the girl you picked up in the Lamoine last week?'

'No.'

'Did you see her at any other time than the one you gave her the ride?'

'No.'

'Have you been in communication with any Anacaon?'

'No.'

'Right,' he said, reaching under his lapel to switch off his concealed recorder. 'You're probably clean. You can stop being a suspect and join the good guys just as soon as Charlot is convinced.' He stepped back, and one of his cronies opened the door. Denton went out and I followed him. The other two didn't join us.

'Are they going to search my room?' I asked incredulously.

'That's right.'

'Hell's bloody wheels. What have I done to deserve all this attention?'

'Played the boy scout when you shouldn't have. You've put yourself on the spot. That girl has disappeared. People think you might have something to do with it, as you haven't been much in evidence lately.'

So much for the quiet life.

Charlot was blazing mad, but not much of it was directed at me. He, at least, thought I was clean. It's nice to know that someone has faith in you. Denton, it seemed, was just eliminating me for the record.

'How did she do it?' asked Charlot, more of Denton than of me. 'How did she get on board a ship at the port? How can two aliens smuggle themselves off *New Alexandria*?'

'Where did they go?' I asked.

'I don't know,' he snapped. 'We haven't even found out where they went *from* yet.'

'Who was the other one?' I asked.

'One of the women on the project. Not an important part of it. She didn't work with us. She was concerned with administrative liaison. If I find out that you had anything to do with this, Grainger, I'll break you.'

'You know I didn't,' I told him.

He nodded. He was just letting off a little steam. Even Titus Charlot got steamed up. Sometimes.

But for what? I wondered.

'Pardon me,' I said, 'but what's the big flap all about? These Anacaona are free agents, aren't they? There's nothing to stop them leaving New Alexandria, is there?'

My suspicious mind began to awake at last.

'This is kidnap,' put in Denton. 'The woman wasn't the girl's mother. She had no right to take her away. And wherever they are they've gone in secret.'

'Even so,' I said, 'are we just concerned about the inconvenience, or what? Why is there such a panic on?'

'I've got years of work tied up in that girl,' said Charlot. 'It'll set the project back half a lifetime.' He was talking half to himself, half to me.

'Oh great,' I said. 'She was just a little girl, was she? Tyler and Lanning only wanted to take her home before it got late, huh? You bastard. What in hell are you *doing* out at that colony?'

'Don't be a fool,' he said. 'The girl is important because I've been conducting a careful and unobtrusive study of her development since the day she was born. A lot of the effort of the colony is going into making the study as complete and as unobtrusive as possible. You know full well that to achieve the kind of synthesis I'm trying to form I need more than knowledge. I need empathy. The Anacaona are very difficult people to understand. We encounter difficulties in translation. The programming of the whole project is threatened if we can't find the core of an understanding. I was looking to that girl to provide me with that core. We haven't interfered with her in any way at all. The whole point of the study would have been defeated if we had. We need that girl.'

It didn't sound too convincing to me. I had the feeling that I wasn't getting the whole truth.

'It's still kidnap,' said Denton, trying to help out—feeling, no doubt, that we'd been sidetracked into irrelevancy.

'The Laws of New Rome allow anybody to leave any world for any reason they choose,' I said.

'Not with somebody else's child they don't,' he said.

'You want to go after her,' I said, suddenly realising why I'd been roped into the heart of the operation. 'You're just hanging about until you find out which ship she left on and where she's bound.'

'We have a good idea already where she's bound,' said Charlot, 'but it would be best to stop her before she gets there, if possible.'

'Why?' I asked. 'Wherever she lands, she'll still be a criminal, if you can prove kidnap.'

'Not on Chao Phrya,' said Charlot. 'The authorities there are uncooperative.'

'Not again,' I complained, despairingly. 'Not another LWA world?'

'Not quite,' he said. 'Not from our point of view. From theirs. The situation on Chao Phrya is difficult and complicated. It won't be easy dealing with them.'

'And you want me to help.'

'I may need more than help,' he said. 'If the woman and Alyne—that's the child—reach Chao Phrya, you might have to go down and fetch her on your own. I don't think they'll let me land.'

'Why?' I asked, fascinated. 'What did you do?'

'A diplomatic failure,' he said obliquely. 'That's not important at all. What is...?'

He was interrupted by the bleeping of his desk phone. He paused to answer it. He listened intently for several moments—the call-circuit was tight-beamed so I couldn't hear what was coming out of the speaker. I watched Charlot's face turn grim, and I could imagine his teeth grinding. Something was upsetting him, and I could see that someone was going to suffer for it. I got the crazy notion that the bogeys might have found something in my room, but I quashed it. Who would want to frame me?

Eventually, he switched off the circuit, and he looked up at us again. He waited a moment or two, stony-faced, and then he spoke.

'You were right,' he said to Denton. 'They had inside help. Tyler's missing too. *Tyler*, the damn fool. I'll make damn sure he never gets to spend it, wherever he is.'

'He'll head for Penaflor,' I suggested helpfully. 'They don't like New Alexandrians on Penaflor.'

Charlot ignored me. He didn't change his expression, nor did he inject anything into his voice, but I'd never before seen him radiate such powerful emotion. '*Wherever* he is,' he repeated.

He turned to Denton. 'Find him,' he said. And then, to me: 'The *Hooded Swan* lifts in two hours. Get ready. Socoro's on board. The captain and I will join you as soon as possible.'

'Nick's on Earth,' I said.

'I know that,' he said testily. 'Miss Lapthorn will be acting captain. You didn't think you'd get the job, did you?'

The nastiness in his voice was quite unimportant and unnecessary. The news was enough to curl *me* up.

Denton left with me.

'How come you get in on all the big secrets?' I asked him. 'Are you really the chief of police masquerading as a hireling?'

'No,' he said. 'I'm Charlot's bodyguard.'

'Bloody hell,' I said. 'I didn't even know he had a bodyguard. Does he need one?'

'Not much,' said Denton. 'At least, he doesn't think so. But while he's on planet he has to be looked after. Same applies to all the other top Library personnel. New Alexandria values its people very highly.'

'But you only guard him when he's here?'

'I'm a cop,' he said, 'not a private bodyguard.'

'Strikes me,' I said, 'that he's an awful lot more vulnerable offworld than on.'

Denton shrugged. 'We can only do so much. He doesn't like his body being guarded. In a way, it's a bum job, because he won't let me close enough to be effective, but if somebody bumps him off while I'm standing around on the wrong corner, I carry the can.'

'Great,' I said. So that was why he spent so much of his time helping walls to stand up straight.

Then another thought struck me. 'Say,' I said. 'Suppose, just for the sake of argument, that there was something going on at that colony. Something against the Law of New Rome? Where are you then?'

'You're imagining things,' he said.

'You mean that Charlot is above the law?'

'That's not what I mean at all.'

'Now there,' I said, 'is what I call hypocrisy. Do you mean to say that if I gave you evidence that Charlot was breaking the law, you'd act?'

'Show me the evidence,' he stalled.

'I might just be able to do that,' I said. 'There's something about this kidnap business that smells. It makes no sense.'

'Yeah?' said Denton, not sounding too convinced, or even interested. 'Well, I tell you what, I'll buy you a drink the night you get back from Chao Phrya, with or without the girl. And you can tell me what happened. And then we'll see who gets to say "I told you so." Okay?'

'You reckon that Charlot's told us the story straight?'

'That's what I reckon.'

'Okay,' I said. 'It's a deal.' I chalked up the date in my mental agenda. I don't often get a chance to say 'I told you so' to a cop.

All cops with purposeful strides are optimists.

CHAPTER FOUR

IF I WERE ASKED TO prepare a list of lady captains I have known and loved, the list would not be very long. In fact, I would be hard pressed to come up with any candidates at all. This does not mean that any fairminded man (or woman) would automatically name me as male-chauvinist-pig-of-the-year. I am myself a fairminded man, and I assess captains on their ability to captain. Personally, I am a good captain. Eve Lapthorn as a captain was a joke. A poor joke.

If he hadn't been angry, I think Titus Charlot would have enjoyed the jump from New Alexandria to Chao Phrya. As it was, nobody was happy in the control room, and Johnny was only happy because he wasn't in the control room. I have rarely seen anyone look quite so uncomfortable as Eve did as she passed out routine orders for the lift. To make the best of the situation for both of us she should have gripped it hard in both hands and maintained a poker-face, but she wasn't up to it. She let her uneasiness and her reluctance show. It helped me to stay irritated. Eve always had a tendency to get on my nerves by virtue of her having been related to the late and much-lamented Lapthorn who had been my friend and partner when *I* had been a captain.

Failing the stone-faced approach, I reckoned that the best thing she could do was to turn down the job. She wasn't tied to Charlot by a slave-chain, and she sure as hell didn't need the money. But I think she regarded it as some kind of challenge, issued not only by Charlot but also by me. Personally, I don't think people should accept challenges which they aren't up to answering, but other people just don't have my keen sense of probability and responsibility in these matters.

The atmosphere aboard the *Hooded Swan* was, as usual, very strained. Perhaps even more so than usual.

In all honesty, I can't say that I remember the *Hooded Swan* as ever having been a happy ship. I enjoyed flying her. I loved sitting inside the hood. But you can never quite forget what's going on behind the control cradle when trouble is just as likely to start there as outside. Every time I grooved her, no matter when or where, I always had to come back to that same air of simmering mistrust and hostility. It didn't even matter whether or not Charlot was there in person. He was always there in spirit.

While I was lifting the *Swan* from Corinth port, I was thinking seriously that the best trip I'd ever taken in the bird was the lunatic drive back through the Halcyon Drift after plundering (or failing to plunder) the *Lost Star*. It had been deadly dangerous and extremely painful, but at least it had been the bird and the wind and myself united against the forces of nature, instead of the wind and myself separately suspended in a sea of negative feeling, which was what I would inevitably find when I had set her in a groove for Chao Phrya. I inspected the charts with all my usual care and precision, and plotted a perfect minimum groove. I almost wished that I had a couple of clouds to nurse her through or a close passage where she might get sucked out of the groove or fluttered within it. But there was nothing but nothing in between New Alexandria and Chao Phrya. There was a lot of it, because Chao Phrya was a long way from the core, but we didn't have to go anywhere near the galactic heart or the frayed fringes of starspace. It was all very nice and safe and boring.

Eve had a cup of coffee ready for me when I peeled off the hood and left the *Swan* to make her own way at a furious, but quite safe, fifty thou. Charlot wanted all possible speed, but at fifty thou we could outrun anything in the galaxy and still have hours in hand when we got to Chao Phrya, thirty hours' start or no thirty hours' start. I thanked her kindly, and didn't make any sarcastic remarks about captains doubling as tea-girls.

'What's the ETA?' demanded Titus.

'Nineteen hours and a bit, I guess,' I told him. 'I can give you the nearest half-second if you like.'

'What about the *White Fire*?' asked Johnny, his voice emanating from the open speaker over the cradle. The *White Fire* was the ship on which the woman and the girl were travelling.

'She can't possibly reach the system until four hours after we make the drop,' I said. 'No trouble at all.'

Charlot laughed humourlessly.

'You're expecting trouble?' I asked him.

'Perhaps,' he said.

'Don't you think you'd better tell us about it?' said Eve, trying to sound as if she was in charge.

'Chao Phrya is a difficult world to deal with'

'So you've said,' I said drily, remembering that he was *persona non grata* there.

'Why?' asked Eve.

'The *Zodiac* families are unfriendly,' he said.

'Go on,' I said, as he paused. 'Tell her the rest. Tell her Chao Phrya is LWA.'

'Chao Phrya is not covered by the principle of Let Well Alone,' said Charlot acidly. 'The Law of New Rome applies on the surface. It's simply that the people who colonised the world don't like outworlders coming in. They permit no further immigration. Except for half a dozen representatives of New Rome they won't even allow embassies from other worlds. They won't trade, they won't even communicate unless they're forced to.'

'Nobody's forced to communicate,' I put in.

'Be quiet,' said Eve. 'Let's hear this.'

She was gaining confidence, but she obviously lacked enthusiasm. But I did as I was told.

'The law requires that the spaceport carry out certain duties with respect to ships in orbit,' said Charlot. 'There are certain circumstances under which they cannot refuse permission to land. As time does not permit us to get the full force of the law behind us before the *White Fire* gets into the system, there may be trouble here. But the restriction should apply equally to both ships. We should both be in orbit when the legal apparatus does manage to get the appropriate messages through to Chao Phrya.'

'Optimist,' I commented.

Nobody took any notice.

'The reason that the people of Chao Phrya adopt these awkward conventions with respect to outworlders is because they are neurotic isolationists,' said Charlot. 'Not one of them has ever left the planet. They have no ships of their own except the *Zodiac*, and that's a shrine now, not a ship. They built the port solely to control all communication with the outworlds.'

'How can they *all* be neurotic?' asked Eve.

'Simple,' I said, jumping in to steal Charlot's big line. 'The *Zodiac* was a generation ship.'

Eve didn't understand. Johnny didn't say a word, but I knew he was still listening, and that he didn't understand either.

'Promised Land,' I said, my voice reflecting my distaste.

'What?'

'Before Spallanzani invented the phase-shift, and long before mass-relaxation, they had spaceships powered by something they called the thrust-cycle process,' I told her. 'You probably know them under the name 'tumblers'—if they teach you any sort of theory at school these days you'll know why. There was space travel before this new and enlightened age of high velocities, you know.'

'Subcee drive,' she said. 'But....'

Charlot took over the explanation again. He was better at it anyway. 'It took the *Zodiac* four hundred and eighty years to travel from Earth to Chao Phrya. They couldn't travel at anything like light-speed. Chao Phrya was in the fifth system which they searched for habitable worlds. They turned down two worlds where they could have survived, because they weren't looking for survival. They were looking for a garden of Eden. A paradise planet. A Promised Land. During all the time that the people lived on that ship—nineteen generations—they supported themselves with promises. They weren't living for themselves at all, but for their descendants. The only purpose in their lives was to give their children a perfect world. That purpose had to be strong. Living aboard a generation ship is not a good life. Eventually, they found that world, and their children inherited it. But the children also inherited the sense of purpose. Inevitably, their attitude to Chao Phrya was the same as their ancestors'. It was the Promised Land. Sacred Soil. Marked down to them and to no others; all they were entitled to want and need for all eternity. It's a common syndrome. It wears off, but not for several generations. In a way, the children of the *Zodiac* were immensely fortunate in that the world they finally found was still undiscovered. It was well within the rim. But civilisation had gone toward the heart, ignoring a lot of worlds *en route*. Chao Phrya was discovered by the galactic civilisation only forty years ago—less than a century after the *Zodiac* had landed.

'Perhaps you can imagine the reactions of the children of the *Zodiac*. They had a tradition of twenty-two generations of sacrifice. Now here were these people flitting about the stars with virtually no effort at all, calmly ignoring what the *Zodiac* people still thought to be immutable Laws of Nature—the quaint old ideas of relativity. Their immediate reaction was to shut themselves off totally—to ignore the galaxy and forget the rest of the human race. But that couldn't be permitted. They had to accept the Law of New Rome. They were offered no choice. Because of the Anacaona.

'To the children of the *Zodiac*, you understand, the Anacaona were just part of the Promised Land package. It simply couldn't occur to any of the *Zodiac* people that the Anacaona had any sort of right to this planet. They were here, but that only meant that they had been provided by a benign providence for the convenience of the children of the *Zodiac*. They weren't people.

They were slaves. So the families—still administered by the crew, who simply became the government of the New World—just moved in and took over. They eradicated virtually all traces of the native culture within hundreds of miles of their landing point, and they were expanding at a frightening rate when the world was rediscovered. There had been no bloodshed—the Anacaona had been conquered without a blow. They were extremely amenable to being conquered. If the rediscovery had been a hundred years later, there might not have been a single wild Anacaon left on the planet. The entire species would have been domesticated and humanised. The Anacaona were intelligent and imitative—the perfect slaves. They had a limited continental range, too. Their own expansion as a species hadn't really got under way.

'The *Zodiac* people were in no danger of committing actual genocide, but they came perilously close to cultural genocide. New Rome sent representatives out, and so did New Alexandria. The quarrel lasted for years. I was sent out during its final stages, to make arrangements for the Anacaon project which has been going on at the colony near Corinth. There's no point in going over all the details of the diplomatic war. You can imagine the difficulties. The children of the *Zodiac* were eventually persuaded that they had no choice. If they didn't let the Anacaona alone, New Rome would move in troops. If Chao Phrya wasn't to be run under the Law of New Rome by the *Zodiac* crew, then it would be run under the Law of New Rome by a military authority. There was no question of Let Well Alone. That principle only applies to alien worlds which don't want to be colonised and human worlds where there are no other considerations to be taken into account but the eccentricities of the particular humans involved.

'The crew had to capitulate. They agreed to handle their world our way, provided that we let them get on with it. If anything, the rediscovery reinforced their determination to remain isolated and free from interference.

'The children of the *Zodiac* hate us. It will wear off in time.

It is wearing off. But we—New Rome and New Alexandria particularly—came and trampled all over their sacred Promised Land and told them how they would have to run it if they didn't want it taken away from them. All that hatred is going to work against us down there. The only thing which will work in our favour is the fact that the only thing the *Zodiac* people are afraid of is the possibility of our coming back to carry out our threats. They'll have to cooperate with us, but we'll have to threaten them in order to make them. They'll be as difficult as they can contrive to be without actually getting us killed or refusing point-blank to help us in accordance with the law.

'I don't think they'll let me land. They might not let more than one of us land in any case, in which case it will have to be you.'

He meant me.

'Thanks a lot,' I said.

'Whatever you do,' he said, 'don't let them think that the whole galaxy isn't behind you. Don't ever suggest for a moment that if they don't do as we say they'll get away with it. We have to make this look like a diplomatic incident of the highest order. The New Romans on planet will back us up. They know the score. But don't give the *Zodiac* people an inch.'

'That's wonderful,' I said. 'I might have to go down there on my own. To a world where every man hates me. Great.'

It didn't really worry me all that much. It looked like the sort of thing I could handle. I only get into difficulties when the situation demands that I be nice to people.

Charlot, on the other hand, was very worried. He was nursing a lot of bitterness about Chao Phrya. I could afford to be philosophical about the sad story he'd just told us. It's a big galaxy. Things go wrong. People are always getting hurt. When cultures collide, someone always suffers. But there's never any way back to square one. These things happen. Too bad.

Being philosophical and cynical about things doesn't make them any better, though. Charlot couldn't be cynical and philosophical, because he saw his purpose in life—the purpose of all human life—in making things better. He was unalterably committed to New Alexandria (just as the colonists were unalterably committed to their Promised Land), and he could never afford to shrug his shoulders. He had tremendous faith in New Alexandria as an instrument of his brand of good.

I don't believe in any brand of good, and I have dire suspicions about New Alexandria, and even direr ones about New Rome. It's not only generation ships which give rise to the Promised Land syndrome, and at least the children of the *Zodiac* would eventually be able to take a practical view of existence. I doubted that New Alexandria and New Rome would ever change. Sacred ideas are always more difficult to reify than sacred soil. I can't help thinking that New Alexandria might be the biggest cultural genocide machine of all time. No matter how sincere its concern for the alien races of the galaxy, its philosophy is unavoidably anthropocentric. Its precepts are human and its methods are human. It's some comment on the New Alexandrian Way that the much-vaunted synthesis of human and Khormon intellectual heritages resulted in a big step forward on *human* technology. No Khormon, so far as I knew, was flying a *Hooded Swan*. I didn't want to argue any of this with Charlot. I think my way, for me. We could never even have compared ideas on a sensible basis. But I knew that if he sent me down alone to the surface of Chao Phrya, I wouldn't be able to throw myself wholeheartedly into his mission. He knew it too. I just don't believe in *Homo galacticus*, much less in *Homo deus*. That's the way it is.

Meanwhile, back at the plot, Eve and I had both caught on to the dimensions of the problem by now. We could look forward to trouble just as much as Charlot.

'What do they think of the colony, down there on Chao Phrya?' I asked.

'They hate the very idea,' said Charlot.

'So what reception are they likely to offer to the woman and the girl?'

'I don't know,' he confessed. 'I think they'd prefer to forget that the colony existed. They won't thank anyone for reminding them of it. They won't give the *White Fire* permission to land. There's no possibility of that.'

'But that's not what worries you?' inserted Eve.

'You think they'll go down anyway,' I amplified.

'I hope not,' he said.

'But it makes for a diplomatic mess if they do,' I said.

'Obviously.'

But that wasn't what he was worried about, and I knew it. *His* worries had been betrayed by his insistence that I not let the *Zodiac* mob suspect that the whole weight of New Roman Law might not stamp them flat if they told us to buzz off. What frightened Charlot was the possibility that New Rome might have far more interest in preserving peace than in solving Titus Charlot's problems for him. He was afraid that the powers of New Rome might conveniently decide that the evidence of kidnap wasn't sufficient. Diplomatic trouble didn't bother him at all. But he thought that the ground might be cut right out from under his feet if we had to wait for a decision from New Rome and if the *Zodiac* people managed to put in a strong protest. I could see why he was willing to let me go down on my own, if there proved to be no other immediate alternative.

For once, he had more faith in me than in the Law of New Rome.

I was flattered. But not enthusiastic. Despite the fact that I had some slight personal involvement in the situation, I was happy to let things get along in their own sweet way.

The transfer at Chao Phrya, nineteen hours and no sleep later, was smooth and routine. Johnny's handling of the engine was getting better all the time. He'd never faced real difficulty, of course, but I could tell that he had some kind of sensitivity. Not the flair of a Rothgar, by any means, but he was an engineer of sorts.

I went into a conventional orbit and began to hail the port. At first, there was no answer at all, but I kept beeping. Eventually, my signal was recognised and a decidedly hostile voice invited me to go ahead.

'This is the *Hooded Swan*,' I told him, and I reeled off our identification codes. I could imagine his hostility growing as he found that we were from New Alexandria. Assuming he could understand the codes, of course.

'What do you want?' he demanded bluntly, before I'd quite finished.

I completed the legal requirements, and then turned away from the console. 'Captain,' I called, in sweet and deadly tones, 'I think you'd better take over.'

Eve moved to the duplicate communications panel in the rear of the control room. She didn't even glance at me.

'What do I tell him?' she asked Charlot. At least, I thought, she didn't just let him take over. It was her job, and she was doing it.

'Tell him the truth,' said Charlot. It seemed like an adventurous policy, but I knew that Charlot was talking about *his* brand of truth, which wasn't quite the same as mine.

'The truth,' I muttered, exhibiting my disgust.

'Keep out of this,' said Eve, with some asperity.

She identified herself formally to the man on the ground, and repeated her own codes.

'What do you want?' repeated the waspish voice from the speaker.

'In a matter of hours,' she said calmly, 'the phaseshift yacht *White Fire* will arrive here. She is under charter to an Anacaon from the colony on New Alexandria. The woman is charged with the crime of kidnapping. Her victim is with her. We want to recover both of them. We ask permission to land, and to place the personnel on board the *White Fire* under arrest as soon as that ship lands.'

'You aren't a police boat.'

'We have the power of arrest. We have the owner aboard, and he has the full authority of the government of New Alexandria.'

The man on the ground should have asked for full identification, but he didn't. The mere mention of New Alexandria was enough to switch on his glands.

'Wait,' he said. 'Maintain your orbit. I'll refer your request to the proper authorities.' I could almost *feel* the sneer in his voice.

He closed the circuit.

'Nice man,' I commented.

We waited. It was a long wait. Either the *Zodiac* people were holding a big debate or the little guy was having a lot of trouble finding his proper authorities. It was well over an hour later when our circuit beeped again. I let Eve answer it.

They didn't waste time on any formalities.

'Permission to land is refused,' said a deep voice. It wasn't the same man we'd spoken to before, unless he was trying to sound more important.

I could see Charlot's teeth gritting.

'Why?' asked Eve.

'We do not acknowledge any New Alexandrian authority,' said the voice firmly, as if all argument would be useless.

'Tell him the law insists we be recognised,' said Charlot quietly.

'The law...,' began Eve, before the voice cut the circuit.

She began beeping him instantly.

He switched back on and said, 'The law is a matter for the officers of the law. We will discuss the matter only with a duly constituted authority.'

'We have such authority,' said Eve coldly. 'If you care to check the codes which we gave you, you will find that we are recognised by New Rome.' She meant, of course, that Charlot was so important New Rome would back him to the hilt. The plain fact was that we *weren't* cops, and they had every right to wait for the cops to arrive. Which would be a long time after the *White Fire*.

'We should have brought Denton,' I said.

'It wouldn't make any difference,' said Charlot. 'They're just as obliged to accept the request from us as they are from anybody else. Tell them they'll be accessories to the crime if they don't comply with our request.'

Eve told them. They weren't impressed.

'The ship to which you refer,' said the deep voice, 'will be refused permission to land. You will both remain in orbit until an authority capable of dealing with the situation arrives.'

Charlot took the mike from Eve. 'Don't be a fool,' he said. 'You can't leave this problem up here in space. The *White Fire* won't ask permission. We demand to be allowed to follow her down and effect an arrest.'

'That is not legal,' said the man on the ground.

Out of the corner of my eye, I could see Charlot's fingernails digging into his palms.

'Will you arrest the crew and passengers aboard the *White Fire* if that ship lands on Chao Phrya?' asked Charlot, holding his temper in.

'Depends where they land, doesn't it?' said the man with the deep voice, with insulting carelessness. 'We don't have anything capable of circumnavigating the planet in a matter of minutes. If he comes down a couple of thousand miles away, there's nothing we can do about it, is there?'

'*We* can!' said Charlot.

'You have no authority so to do,' returned the man on the ground. 'You must maintain orbit.'

And he switched off again.

This time, nobody bothered to try and recall him. We'd heard what he had to say. There was no point in arguing until we had something to argue about. We could reopen negotiations if and when we had a fait accompli to present them with. There was nothing we could do but wait for the *White Fire* and hope against hope that her captain wouldn't be anticipating trouble and would go down to the port, or at least to where some member of the *Zodiac* police force could get to her.

I didn't really feel lucky.

CHAPTER FIVE

ABOUT TEN MINUTES BEFORE the *White Fire* was due to show, Eve told me to get back inside the hood and fuse my eyesight with the *Swan*'s perceptors so that I could report what happened. I obeyed without a word.

Nobody can see spaceships with the naked eye, except at point-blank range, but the *Swan* had much better eyes than the feeble ones we carry in our heads. She was so sensitive she could pick up a pea at ninety million miles (though the images she got from distant objects were necessarily a bit behind the times) and her computers could run a fast sort which could separate irrelevant lumps of rock from interesting items in a matter of microseconds. All the relevant information registered automatically with the organometallic synapses in the console, and were made available inside the hood at a direct sensory level. There's no way to explain what things look like or feel like inside an ordinary ship's hood, let alone the *Hooded Swan*'s. It's an experience like no other. The outcome of the whole process was that I was able to 'see' the *White Fire* as soon as she passed the orbit of the fifth planet (Chao Phrya was the second) and I watched her come all the way in. She'd made transfer to zero-phase a long way out, and she was in no hurry.

I could see her, and she could see me. I think her captain must have guessed what ship we were.

She was dead on schedule, allowing a few minutes for the distant p-shift. It was no surprise—she'd come along pretty much the same groove we had and there was nothing in the way but hard vacuum.

'She's coming in right now,' I said. 'Do you want me to hail her or move the *Swan* into her way?'

'Hail her,' said Charlot.

I beamed a beep at her. 'Do you want me to identify myself if and when she answers?' I asked him.

'Might as well,' he said. 'He'd be a fool if he didn't know.'

When the beep elicited no immediate response I stepped up the power and gave it a full frequency register so that he couldn't tune it out. I didn't see any reason not to be rude.

He answered, and said, 'Hello.'

'This is the *Hooded Swan*....,' I began.

'Surprise, surprise,' he said.

'You're under arrest,' I said, cutting out the formalities, and trying to sound like Denton.

'Don't get in my way,' he said. 'You may be fast and slick, but you can't stop me. Just don't try.'

I put my hand over the mike.

'More whiz-kids,' I commented to Charlot, with a hint of bitterness. 'What do you want me to do?'

'What did you expect?' he replied. 'It takes a real lunatic to accept a criminal run out of New Alexandria. He's no real spaceman.' I didn't bother reacting to that, though I'd known a good many real spacemen in my time who'd have relished the thought of a bent run out of New Alexandria. While I couldn't say that most of my best friends had been kidnappers, not a lot of them would have turned up their nose at big money.

'What shall I do?' I demanded to know.

'Watch him,' said Charlot.

'You don't want me to crowd him?'

'No.'

I watched him. There wasn't much to watch. I knew pretty much what was going to happen, and it happened.

'He's going in,' I reported. 'He hasn't even paused to beep the ground.'

'Where's he going to land?' asked Charlot. I could feel the

anger in his voice.

'I can't tell,' I said. 'He's going the wrong way around. I'll have to turn to watch him down. Otherwise the planet'll be between us'

'Well, turn, then,' snapped Charlot.

I took the *Swan* out of orbit and followed the *White Fire* along her decaying trajectory.

'Do you want me to land?' I asked.

There was a pause. It was a difficult decision. He settled for the legal way.

'No,' he said. 'Note her position. Then get back to the orbit. Then get me that fool on the ground.'

I complied.

Embarrassing minutes dragged by while I beeped the spaceport. I was afraid I'd have to pull the same trick that I'd pulled on the captain of the *White Fire* to force an acknowledgement out of them. But they knew what was happening as well as we did. They knew they had to reopen talks.

'Come on,' muttered Charlot—a most unusual gesture of impatience.

'They're probably still tracking the *White Fire*,' I said. 'It'll take them longer to work out her position than it took us. They have inferior equipment.'

'Even *they* can track a ship,' snarled Charlot. 'How far away from them is she?'

'She's a hell of a long way from the ground signal,' I said. 'Maybe sixteen hundred miles, in an area of uniform green that must be eight hundred miles across. Rain forest. Must be.'

Charlot was at my elbow by now, peering at the console. I couldn't see him, because I had the hood on, but I knew he was there.

Ground opened up the circuit.

'Thanks a lot,' I said. 'This is the *Hooded Swan* again.'

'I know who it is,' said the deep voice. 'What do you want now?'

'You know bloody well what we want,' I said. 'The *White*

Fire just went down.'

'That's our problem,' he said.

I knew that Charlot wanted to take over, so I peeled the hood off and waved him to go ahead.

'Identify yourself,' demanded Charlot. 'Give your rank and name.'

'This is Lieutenant Delgado of the *Zodiac* crew,' came the reply.

'Well, you listen to me, *Lieutenant*,' he said. 'This is Titus Charlot of New Alexandria, and you'd better find me someone with a whole lot more authority to talk to. If you don't know what my name means I suggest that you check with the embassy from New Rome. I want the captain, but if you can't get him in a hurry get me whoever you can. I want to talk to someone *now* who can get something *done*. And when you've got him, get the New Rome authority and someone from the families as well. This is something you can't handle and you'd better believe that.'

That's the sort of approach which almost invariably works when dealing with military types. The Lieutenant wasn't real military, of course, but rank is rank and the *Zodiac* crew still functioned like a crew.

'The proper authorities have been informed,' said Delgado serenely. 'Representatives from New Rome are being consulted. You will be informed in due course of the decision which has been taken.'

'Now just you wait a minute, Delgado,' said Charlot, drawing a deep breath.

'Careful, Titus,' I murmured. 'Your humanity is showing.'

He ignored me. 'You are toying with the future of your people,' he said to Delgado. It seemed a bit strong to me, but Charlot was pulling all the stops out. Half measures weren't going to get a look-in. He was determined to carry this one by simple bluster. 'If you don't know that a kidnapper using your planet as a refuge spells big trouble then you have no right to be at the other end of this circuit,' he said. 'You have refused us permission to apprehend a known criminal, and you have failed to do so yourselves. The *White Fire* will lift inside five minutes, and that makes you the accessory to a crime. With your co-operation we could have ended this whole affair, but you've contrived to turn it into a diplomatic incident. We demand your co-operation now in tracking down the kidnapper and the victim. Now get off this circuit and give me someone who's empowered to give me that co-operation.'

Strong stuff.

A new voice issued from the speaker.

'This is Commander Hawke of the *Zodiac*,' it said. 'Your official request is noted. We have no evidence that any crime has been committed. We had not, and have not, any grounds for apprehending the *White Fire*. The ship had no permission to land, but that is entirely our affair and we intend taking no action. When we have been approached by the proper authorities we will consider your request for assistance in this matter. Permission to land is refused.'

Sock it to 'em, son, I thought. Don't be railroaded. Stick up for your rights. I didn't say a word out loud lest my loyalties be questioned.

'This is Titus Charlot of New Alexandria,' said Charlot. 'I am the administrator of the Anacaon colony on New Alexandria. The security of that colony is my sole responsibility. I have the legal right to demand that you give me all possible assistance in carrying out my responsibilities toward the members of that colony. One of them has been kidnapped and the kidnapper is currently at large on your world. This situation is due entirely to your lack of co-operation. If you do not immediately review your position and give us all the help we need I will request official intervention by the Law Enforcement Agencies of New Rome.'

As he stopped, he glanced at me, and I could see the glitter in his eye. He thought he was winning.

I thought he was winning, too, unless Hawke could come back just as strong.

But Hawke had faltered. He was thinking instead of holding fast.

'Can you give us proof of what you say?' he demanded.

'It can be proven,' said Charlot.

'Then prove it.'

'We are in possession of a warrant for the arrest of the Anacaon woman known as Lenah, late of the New Alexandrian colony.'

'The warrant comes from New Rome?' Hawke queried, knowing damn well it didn't.

'The warrant was issued in full accordance with the Law of New Rome,' said Charlot firmly.

There was another pregnant pause. 'The woman will be arrested,' said Hawke finally.

'When?'

'As soon as possible.'

'That's not good enough. A girl has been kidnapped. A child. We demand the immediate mounting of a search party, and we further demand that our personnel should accompany that party. We demand that all possible resources be brought to bear.'

'They will be,' said Hawke, offhandedly. 'But we cannot accede to your request to land.'

'You'd better,' said Charlot, unpleasantly and succinctly, 'or I'll have a New Roman cruiser here with six hundred troops.'

That was a big lie, and I knew it. But did Hawke? And what would the New Roman Embassy have to say about the magnitude of such a threat, coming, as it did, from an administrator of the Library?

'You'll have to wait,' said Hawke sharply.

'How long?' said Charlot, reluctant to let it go.

'You'll have your answer within the hour,' he said.

'Make it twenty minutes,' said Charlot.

'One hour,' said Hawke. 'You are ordered to wait.' He put a faint but definite stress on the word 'ordered.'

The circuit snapped shut.

'I don't think you handled that very well,' I told Charlot

'I don't care what you think,' he replied. He was still mad.

'I could have done it better myself,' I remarked, trying to needle him. I'd probably never have another opportunity.

But he shut up tight. The long wait began again.

I was tired.

Better not lean on him, counselled the wind. All kinds of things might happen yet. If this doesn't come off, the last thing you want is for him to blame you.

He can't blame me, I said.

Just don't give him the chance, he said. Remember just who has to look after Charlot's end on the planet, if you ever *do* get down. He won't be doing any legwork in the jungle himself, no matter how important this issue is to him.

That, of course, was true.

Ah, I said, we'll never get down there. They aren't going to fall for the gunboat threat.

They don't know any better, he said.

And he was right about that, too.

I continued to talk to him, to while away the time, but we didn't have anything of vital importance to discuss. I was just trying to keep my attention alive against the declining effect of my last stimshot. I didn't know whether I ought to take another or not. Whether we landed within the hour or were condemned to stay up forever, the chances of getting to sleep soon looked reasonably good.

The conversation drifted away from the issue at hand to other less memorable and less relevant affairs. The conversation was not unpleasant, but it is perhaps more important to record that it was not purposeful. It was idle chatter, nothing more. That's some measure of the bonhomie which we'd cultivated of late. The constant stress and strife of the caves of Rhapsody had been left behind in those caves, along with the infernal darkness. It no longer seemed to matter quite so much that the wind was by no means impotent in physical terms. It had seemed a matter of tremendous importance while we'd been in the caves, but it didn't seem tremendous now. I was coming round to measuring him by what he said and what he did rather than by what he was potentially capable of doing. I was reasonably sure that he posed no meaningful threat to my beloved egocentricity and independence of spirit. There has to come a time when you stop fighting things and learn to live with them. It was getting to be that way with the wind. The transition from one attitude to the other had not been abrupt, but it had been considerable. I was forming the opinion that if the wind was changing me at all, then he was changing me for the better. The wind, of course, had told me so all along, but he was too polite to remind me now.

At the end of the hour, Commander Hawke came back on to the circuit and told us we could land. He also told us that we could have the full co-operation of the *Zodiac* crew in following up the matter of the illegal landing of the *White Fire* and its human cargo.

On one condition.

Even that was better than we had expected, from Charlot's point of view. Instead of only one of us being able to join the search, they would accept two of us. I stress that this was better from Charlot's point of view. Not from mine. Charlot nominated Eve, and—of course—me.

Captain Eve. And Crewman Grainger.

I knew it was going to be a bad trip.

CHAPTER SIX

IF EITHER OF US THOUGHT that Commander Hawke's capitulation meant that things were destined to go our way, then we were quickly disillusioned. Under pressure, the children of the *Zodiac* permitted us to land. Under pressure, they agreed to mount a search for the people landed by the *White Fire* (the ship itself, of course, had taken off again, and I never expected to hear from her—it's easy enough to change a name and get new papers). Under pressure, they let us join in. All very nice. We appreciated it. Until we found out what their idea of a full-scale search was.

There were two of us. There were also two of them. They were called Max and Linda. They hated each other. Linda was a member of the *Zodiac* crew. She was nominally our liaison officer—to help us in our dealings with the Anacaona. She was supposed to be an anthropologist. She was a nice person, and about as useful as Eve, which wasn't very.

Max was a Family man—he bore the name of two of the most influential of the *Zodiac*'s twelve eugenic units. He was what passed for the Law on Chao Phrya. He wasn't really a policeman—more a kind of fake Texas ranger. His function seemed to be more concerned with making sure that we weren't about to indulge in any subversive activities while we were treading on the sacred soil than rendering us any effective assistance.

We didn't meet Max and Linda until we'd been taken a safe distance away from the port. They didn't want us complaining to Charlot. We weren't allowed our own medical supplies. The Chao Phryans were bent on turning the whole thing into a farce. Charlot's threats had made them shift their ground, all right. But all the bluster had confirmed their absolute determination to make things as difficult as humanly possible while still yielding to our perfectly legal demands.

I was dead sure that I didn't want to go walking around in any jungles under the conditions which the *Zodiac* people were insistent upon, but there was damn little I could do. Eve handled the protests which we distributed liberally almost every minute of the first day we were down, but she got absolutely no change at all. They were doing all they could, and they were doing all we had asked them to do. Take it or leave it.

I would have left it. Eve took it. She thought it was best to try, no matter how poor they insisted on making our chances. I had to take the orders. I knew I could look after myself, and probably after Eve as well, but I wouldn't have bet good money on our chances of success.

Oddly enough, I don't think either of our two indigenous compatriots was in on the big joke. They seemed to take it one hundred percent seriously. They didn't like us, but they were willing to get along with us, and they were honestly optimistic about our chances.

'Don't worry,' said Linda. 'It's only a matter of time. These people can't hide from the Anacaona, wherever they are. The forest people will find them.'

The theory was all very fine. But could we count on the help of the Anacaona? After all, both of the people we were looking for were Anacaona. Why would the forest people give them up to us?

But Linda was most definite about that. 'You don't know the Anacaona,' she told me. 'We can be absolutely sure of their co-operation.'

'How come?' I wanted to know.

'The Anacaona always co-operate,' she told us. She didn't know why, and she couldn't explain it. But she was sure.

Linda Petrosian was about twenty-eight standard years, with dyed silver hair and strong, well-shaped features. She was very handsome, as befitted someone descended from a population which had been eugenically controlled for nineteen generations. She was a devout believer in the Promised Land. She was devoted to the soil and the air and everything that grew or walked on Chao Phrya. She loved it all, because it was hers. Charlot had led me to believe that the crew might be a step back from the ultimate possessiveness of the Families, simply by virtue of the fact that they had a tradition of control over the *Zodiac* story. But Linda's commitment, at least; was no less for that. If anything, she was more fanatical—or prejudiced, since she wasn't violent about it—than I would have expected after a full century plus of life on the surface. She was certainly more dedicated than Max Volta-Tartaglia. Perhaps it was because the crew had the tradition of organisation and responsibility that they clung harder to the prop of faith.

Linda was supposed to be an expert on the Anacaona, but well before the time I set eyes on my first native I knew that she was a very inexpert expert. She loved the Anacaona, honestly and genuinely, but any concept of the Anacaona as a self-contained and self-ordained cultural species was quite beyond her. The Anacaona, so far as she was concerned, were a part of the Promised Land. They had properties and characteristics. She knew a lot about them, but it was all descriptive. She knew no why or how. All her knowledge of the Anacaona wasn't worth a damn, so far as I could see. She was perfectly happy to see them freed from slavery, but she had no conception whatsoever of why New Rome had insisted so urgently that they should be freed. She thought it was because slavery was cruel. She thought that the Anacaona ought to be educated and allowed to take a proper place in the culture of the Promised Land. Human culture. In her own way, she was just as bent on cultural genocide as the landfall generation had been. Only she was killing them with kindness. Her most treasured ambition was to turn the Anacaona into fake human beings with an appropriate depth of devotion and love for the Promised Land.

I could almost like and admire Linda Petrosian, except for the fact that she was not sane.

I could never have liked Max Volta-Tartaglia, any more than he could ever have liked me. He was a practical man. He knew that the universe was a lot bigger than any miserable plot of Promised Land. He knew that the stars weren't just lights in the sky and that they couldn't be treated as such. He hated New Rome and New Alexandria and all outworlders, but he knew that someday his world was going to have to come to terms with them, and he saw no point in remaining wilfully blind to the fact. He didn't want to open the planet, but he did favour an end to vain stupidity and diplomatic farce. He wanted to deal with realities. If only his attitude to the selfsame realities hadn't been so ludicrously and implacably hostile he might have made a lot of sense. As it was, he was a great big pain in the neck. He was amenable to argument and rationality, but he wore the chip on his shoulder as if it was a medal, and he was an out-and-out bastard.

Eve compared him to me a couple of tunes. She could have been just a little bit right, in some respects, but not in the important ones. I am, above all else, a capable man.

Max wasn't.

Time passed very quickly on Chao Phrya. The days were only seventeen hours long. But we were forced to waste so much of that time that my patience was very badly frayed before we had even started on our search.

I found out all of what I've set down so far concerning Max and Linda in a very short space of time. Eve and I were forced to live virtually in their pockets, and they hardly stopped talking for the first three days. They took great pains to explain themselves, and greater pains to explain that they were in no way apologising for themselves or for the attitude that their superiors were taking in handling our problem. They had a genuine desire for us to understand their part in the scheme of things. But they didn't seem to be in any particular hurry to get on with the scheme of things.

Nobody seemed to give any consideration at all to the fact that a little girl had been abducted. Nobody considered that there might be any urgency. The *Zodiac* people were concerned only about us, not at all about the purpose of our mission.

To tell the truth, I found time to wonder about what kind of trouble, if any, the girl might be in. It was very difficult to make any kind of sense out of this supposed crime. It must have taken a great deal of money to set up, and there seemed to be no obvious profit in it for the woman concerned. Baby-snatching is an old crime, of course, but this was a very big baby, and the mechanics of the thing were all wrong. The escape from New Alexandria had been carefully planned. Otherwise, it could never have succeeded.

We began our journey from the port in a jeep. We had only a packsack apiece, so little had we been allowed to bring with us from the *Swan*. We transferred from the jeep to a train, which took us to the capital. I expected to be transferred to some faster form of transport there, so as to get us to the theatre of operations with all due speed, but that was far too optimistic.

For a start, there *was* no faster form of transport available. The Chao Phryans had only short-range planes, and they were all operational at the frontier of *Zodiac* civilisation. A long way away.

On top of that, the *Zodiac* people had no intention of letting us begin our long journey at once. There were formalities. Lots of them. The only time I was ever glad that Eve was along was while we were kicking our heels in the capital. She had to handle the formalities. They must have threatened even her placid temper.

The capital city had been established, naturally enough, on the spot where the *Zodiac* came down. It was one great big show-place. We saw the *Zodiac* and a lot more. We weren't allowed to miss out. The last thing we wanted to be doing was sightseeing, so that was the first thing they made us do. All the while they assured us that there was no trouble, that they were only trying to make things easier, that matters in the forest were well under control, that we could rely on the Anacaona.

Naturally, we complained bitterly. We tried bluff in the same style as Charlot. We ranted and we threatened. But they had made the crucial move when they had restricted Charlot to the ship and refused to let us use our own call-circuit. We weren't big enough to cut any ice. I often wondered what they were telling Charlot about our progress, or lack of it. Probably nothing but inconsequentialities. What could he do but wait, unless he had something definite to complain about?

By the time we actually left the capital (by train) and made tracks toward the forest where the *White Fire* had come down, the Chao Phryans must have had time to check with New Rome. They must have found out more or less where they stood. I don't know how sure they were of their own situation, but they sure as hell didn't give us any better treatment than we'd already come to expect. On the other hand, they didn't leave us to rot in the capital while they did everything themselves. They let us carry on.

The train carried us for one day, and then we took a hovercraft. We covered a lot of miles, travelling all night as well as all day. But it was not until noon of our sixth day (local) on Chao Phrya that we finally reached the edge of the *Zodiac* Families' colonial surge, and actually got a sight of the edge of the rain forest.

We rested that afternoon in a kind of half-town, half-camp. There were more Anacaona around than humans. The Anacaona were still doing a lot of the construction work, though slavery had been abolished forty years before. I wondered how much they were being paid.

Max pointed at the high line of colour which marked the horizon. 'That's it,' he told me. 'Your ship came down somewhere in there. The Anacaona will have picked up anybody who got off. All we have to do is get to the Anacaona.'

'How do we do that?' I wanted to know. I felt sure there had to be another catch.

'Easy,' he said. 'We'll pick up a couple of the tame goldens to guide us. It shouldn't take more than a week.'

'A *week*?' I protested. 'How come?'

'We have to walk,' he said.

'What's wrong with the hovercraft?'

'No good in the jungle.'

'What about helicopters? You do have helicopters here, don't you?'

'Oh yeah,' he said, 'we have helicopters here. But they're no good in the jungle either. Can't see through the canopy from up top. Besides which, the Anacaona can only guide us along the floor. They wouldn't know what to make of it from upstairs.'

I didn't know whether he was giving me real answers or whether he was still being difficult for the sake of it. I didn't really care. It came to the same thing in the end. If Max said we walked, then we walked. No argument.

Unlike some people, I don't exactly feel naked without a gun. On the other hand, I didn't exactly relish the thought of tramping around in a jungle for a week or more without any kind of protection. Max had a gun, of course, and a call circuit, and a medical kit. But Max wasn't what I called protection. I wouldn't trust him as far as I could throw a feather into a headwind. The prospect of what was to come was far from enchanting.

Linda spent the afternoon talking to the Anacaona, looking for information about the search and trying to persuade individuals to act as guides. Apparently, everyone knew about the *White Fire* coming down, and they also knew where. Anybody and his cousin could have taken us to the spot, but that wasn't quite what we needed. We wanted to find two people, not a patch of burnt ground. Most of the natives didn't know anything at all about the forest nomads—they'd been brought here as a labour force by the colonists. But Linda was nevertheless confident that we could find exactly what we needed in the Anacaon village.

While Linda was handling her end of the operation Max found other things to do as well, and for much of the time Eve and I were at a loose end. It was a familiar feeling.

'How much longer is it all going to take?' Eve wanted to know.

'Max reckons a week yet before we find them' I told her. 'Figure another week to get back home. Then refigure in standard instead of this local quicktime. It still comes to a fair number of days'

'Charlot will be angry.'

'Sure he will,' I said. 'So what?'

She didn't feel the need to answer that one.

'Surely it would be easier to locate the forest people using a helicopter,' she said.

I shrugged. 'If they don't give us a copter there's not much we can do except walk,' I said. 'But don't be too quick to put it down to natural cussedness. Take a look at the trees around you.'

She looked. She didn't see anything significant.

'They don't have leaves,' she said finally.

'Too true they don't,' I told her. The trees were equipped with membranous drapes mounted on rubbery branches. To increase their photosynthetic activity they extended the drapes like the pages of a book. 'That trick wouldn't work if the trees were more densely packed,' I pointed out. 'This is open country, but it's probably as close as those trees can grow without having things get in their way. In a jungle, things have to be done differently. All available space has to be used to maximum effect. I think we'll find that inside the rain forest those membranes will be arrayed horizontally rather than vertically. The trees will be like giant umbrellas. The canopy will be just that. I'll lay odds that from up top the jungle is just an expanse of solid green.'

She tried to visualise it.

'What will it be like inside,' she asked. 'On the ground?'

'Dark,' I said.

'And we have to walk around in there for more than a week?'

'Probably be more comfortable,' I said. 'You sleeping well?'

She shook her head, knowing already what I was about to say.

'Circadian rhythms disturbed by the short day,' I said, going ahead anyway. 'In there we might be able to get back to a twenty-four-hour cycle.' This was distinctly optimistic. For one thing there's dark and there's a pitch black, and there's a big difference. For another, all the rest of the party were attuned to a seventeen-hour day, and wouldn't appreciate our wanting to switch to twenty-four for our own convenience.

'Anyway,' I continued, 'I wouldn't worry about little things like walking around in the dark if I were in your position. I'd be much more disposed to worry about all the difficulties which this lot might yet think to throw at us.' And that, of course, was sheer pessimism, just to even the score.

'I don't like this world,' she said feelingly.

'That's the expanding civilised universe for you,' I said, with my customary fatalism. 'This is what worlds are like these days. What do you expect? Your brother didn't like it either. He always used to prefer the rim, and he always liked to deal with the natives direct. He wasn't a man-hater by any means, but he despised the second-stage invaders—the exploiters and the moneymen and the politicians. He liked things simple, not packed and predigested to some fancy recipe. You know the syndrome—primitive man against the elements. The archetypal Western hero.'

'Yes,' she said, 'I know.'

I didn't often talk to her about her brother. It was an uncomfortable issue, ever since the charming discussion we'd had in New York Port about whether or not and to what degree I'd been responsible for his death.

'You felt the same way,' she said, after a few moments' silence.

'Not a lot,' I claimed. 'Mythical man was never my type. I'm no romantic—the hell with Rousseau and the back-to-the-trees boys. I like to spend what I make, and make what I spend. We couldn't do either very well while we were bouncing around on the rim. Sure, sharks bite and I don't like them. But they swim where the pickings are and they're just a hazard of the waters.

There's no point in hating them for it. These days, the universe is shrinking so fast that you have to live with everybody whether you like it or not. You can't find a garden world on which to live out your days. Paradise is a marketable commodity now, and the companies move in, slap on a hefty slice of cosmetic stream-lining and start the auction. They're so good at it, it doesn't even take them a year any more. Instant fairyland—just add money. Sure it's in lousy taste—who ever made money out of aesthetic sensibilities? You can't hide any more. Not anywhere. You have to live where the people live. Compared to the compa-nies the *Zodiac* mob are a bunch of stone-age savages. They haven't anything like the technology that someone like Caradoc can bring to bear. But how long do you think the rain forests are going to last? How long before the colonists have it all? Do you seriously think that the human race is going to leave a single galactic stone unturned? Like hell. So that's the way it is. And you have to live with it. I don't hold it against anybody, and I'm sure as hell not going to spend my time running away from it all to find skinny patches of sand where I can bury my head and pretend to be an ostrich. Okay?'

'Fine,' she said. 'Just fine. You really love people and the great human dream. You're a part of it all. I bet you just love New Alexandria too.'

'Best of all,' I assured her.

'But you like aliens?' she probed. 'You really do like aliens?'

'Sure I do. Some of them. But it's only prejudice. Hell, every-body has prejudice. Ninety percent of people are as proud as can be about their prejudice. Can't I have a little bit as well? I'm only human, when all said and done. I like aliens. I can approach an alien with a clean slate. I don't know anything about him, and I can judge exactly what I see. I can estimate him as I find out what he does and says. But I can't approach a man that way. I know far too much about him already to take him as he comes. Whatever he says, I daren't take on the level. Whatever he does, I have a whole range of possible motives for him. I know men too well, because I am one. I don't like that. I'm a simple man, and I like to be dealing with what I'm seeing and feeling at a particular moment. I don't like to be carrying around a whole bibleful of preconceptions and qualifications that I have to dump on every moment that passes. It squashes the moments dead, see?'

'It doesn't make sense,' she said.

'It makes sense to me,' I told her.

'Do you like the Anacaona?' she asked.

'How do I know?' I complained. 'Do I have to tag everything I see with plus or minus? I don't know anything about the Anacaona. I gave one a ride in my car once. That's all.'

'What about the *Zodiac* people?'

'You have to be joking. The *Zodiac* bunch are completely unlovable. They're going to extremes to make themselves that way. Who am I to argue? If they want to be the biggest bastards in the galaxy, who am I to stand in their way? I think they're making a good job of it. I don't say I haven't known worse people, because I've known people who tried harder. But I concede the *Zodiac*s the proper fruit of their labours. No, I don't like them and I don't want anything to do with them. Now wouldn't they just love that?'

'You don't think that their idea of Promised Land makes sense?'

'Sense?' I queried. 'I didn't say anything about sense. Certainly it makes sense. It's one of the most sensible things I've ever come across. You tell me that the great human surge of conquest, civilisation and culture isn't the Promised Land syndrome. You tell me that New Alexandria isn't playing Promised Land with all creation. You tell me that New Rome isn't playing ideological Promised Land. You tell me that Penaflor and the company belt aren't playing commercial Promised Land. You tell me that the Engelian Hegemony aren't playing Communist Promised Land. The *Zodiac* people are by far and away the most sensible of the lot. They don't want the whole universe. They only want one world. Isn't that more sensible? You always stand a better chance with a narrow mind. It's a fact of life.'

'But you don't hate,' she said, with more than a trace of sarcasm. 'All that and you don't hate. You can mix your venom with all kinds of assurances that you have to live with it all, that it's the way of things and you have to like it.'

'I don't have to like it,' I said. 'I don't have to like it at all.'

'And you don't,' she said. 'Sure, you don't hate people. You have to live with them, don't you? But you hate having to live with them. What's the difference?'

'The difference,' I said, 'is where the hate goes. Nobody else gets hurt by mine. Not by the hate, nor by any crazy ideas I might have like Promised Land.'

'You get hurt,' she said.

'No I don't,' I told her.

'You've set yourself up all alone,' she persisted. 'You've cut yourself off from the whole universe just because other people think it's their playground.'

'That's right,' I said. 'I'm the original alienated man.' I spat out the vital word as if I were spitting acid.

And I'm not alone, I added. Silently. Never again alone.

Two years on Lapthorn's Grave had turned me right off the galaxy and life in general. I never was one for the joys of spring and the spirit of adventure, unlike Lapthorn, but I really had sat fairly comfortably in my chosen slice of life. It was only since coming back that things had achieved their present dark conformation.

Not since you came back, said the wind. Since you went away. You're still living in the shadow of Lapthorn's Grave. If you want to come out of it, you can.

Thanks a lot, I said. Everybody wanted to welcome me back to humanity. I wondered why.

CHAPTER SEVEN

LINDA FOUND US AGAIN about dusk. She had an Anacaon with her. I was still at the stage where they all looked pretty much alike to me, but when I subjected this one to close scrutiny I figured that I would have little enough difficulty remembering him. He had sharp eyes and a lantern-jawed hungry look that seemed quite out of place in a member of such a delicately formed people.

He was slender, like all of his race, and almost seven feet tall, which was a shade above the average for the adult male. He wore a kind of skirt of soft grey material, and an undergarment of similar cloth which was visible at the shoulders. Instead of a jacket he had a strange rigid garment like the breastplate from a suit of armour, made of something hard and chitinous. It was basically grey in colour, but it had some kind of a weird pattern on it—a sulphur-yellow cloud with an uneven purple border. It didn't look like a work of art—more like one of nature's accidents.

'This is Danel,' said Linda. 'He knows the forest as well as anyone, and he says that he can contact the wild Anacaona without any trouble.'

'Good,' said Eve. 'We'll be very grateful for his help.'

Danel was looking around absently while this exchange was going on.

'Does he speak English?' asked Eve, observing his lack of attention.

'No,' she said. 'But I can make myself understood in his dialect. He says that his brother and sister must come with us—his brother speaks good English and his sister can manage simple conversation. I don't know how much Danel understands of what we say, but he never speaks any English.' She glanced sideways at the alien as she made this last remark, as if she mistrusted his claim to speak only his own language.

Danel didn't bat an eyelid.

'Why should he lie about it?' I asked.

'He wouldn't,' said Linda. 'Anacaona don't lie. He just doesn't say anything at all about it, and one can never be sure how much to assume. The Anacaona are a very difficult people to understand.'

I thought at the time she was making excuses for her own failure to understand, but I misjudged her. The Anacaona really were a very difficult people to understand.

Linda and Danel exchanged a few chopped phrases in the click-and-whisper of the Anacaon tongue, and then Linda redirected her attention to us.

'Danel is a spiderhunter,' she said. 'He wants you to know that you will be safe in the forest with him. Otherwise he would not take his sister.'

This calm pronouncement caused me a twinge of fear. This was the first official indication we'd had that the forest wasn't a nice place to go walking. I'd expected it, of course, but it was still not very nice to be right.

'He hunts spiders,' I said calmly, knowing that there was more to come. 'What sort of spiders?'

'They weigh about two tons,' she said.

'That's what I thought,' I said. 'Common, are they?'

'No.'

'That's a relief.' This interjection came from Eve.

'But I'll bet they eat people,' I said.

'If they get the chance,' said Linda.

'Yet the powers-that-be still insist we go in there without weapons?' I said.

'I'm afraid so. But you'll be in no danger.'

'Thanks for the promises,' I said. 'I only hope your people at the top realise how annoyed Titus Charlot will be if two of his hirelings end up cemented to a spider web.'

'They don't build webs,' said Linda.

'Thanks,' I said again. 'I was speaking figuratively.'

'Danel has a gun,' said Linda. 'He also carries an axe, which is the approved instrument for killing them. Max will be armed as well. I don't think you need worry too much.'

'What about the others?'

'Micheal usually hunts with Danel. He carries a musical instrument—'

'Don't tell me,' I interrupted. 'Music has charms to soothe the savage breast. He's a small-town Orpheus, right?'

'Very much so,' she countered serenely. 'The music can attract the spiders or hypnotise them. Micheal holds the spiders in thrall while Danel kills them with the axe. It's almost a ritual.'

'What part does little sister play?' I asked. 'Is she the live bait?'

'Don't be ridiculous,' said Linda. 'Danel and Micheal aren't hunting this trip. Mercede wants to go with them and they see no reason why not. That should reassure you with regard to spiders.'

'Okay,' I said. 'Let's not worry any more in public. Danel looks bored stiff. What do we do now? I don't suppose this dead end has a four-star hotel, so where do we get some sleep before the big safari?'

'We'll stay with Danel,' she said.

Max Volta-Tartaglia had come up behind her while she was speaking.

'Not me,' he said. 'I've got other plans.'

Linda gave him a dirty look, as if she thought he had a duty to go look at her prize Anacaona in their natural setting. He walked away again, completely unconcerned. He didn't invite Eve and myself to share his other plans. I think I would rather have gone with Danel anyhow.

Danel's house was a crude wooden affair, as were the forty or so others which stood near it. What the Anacaona knew about architecture they had obviously learned putting up buildings for the humans. There was no difference whatsoever between shanties *Zodiac*-style and shanties native-style. Outside, the Anacaon dwellings looked faintly ludicrous. Inside, they looked extremely ludicrous.

Imagine an Anacaon in your own front room and you have some idea of the effect that these people were trying to create. There was hardly any evidence of their own racial identity outside their own bodies. They were living human lives.

In the house we met Micheal and Mercede—even the *names* were human, or as nearly so as made no difference—and one or two of the older generation, who also had human names, human mannerisms, and who spoke perfect English.

I understood very little of what went on that night. There was a great deal of talk, before, during and after the lavish meal which they gave us. It seemed to me that the older people were finding themselves to be more human than they wanted themselves to be, but were trying to get along with it, while the younger were pretending to be less human than they were without quite knowing how. This may seem to be a very complicated impression to gain from a fairly simple situation which I admit to not understanding. It is indeed possible, if not probable, that I read this into the situation rather than observing it. I was never sure about the Anacaona. I knew all about the decay of the *Zodiac* slave system in the wake of pressure from New Rome, and I was well aware of the fact that cultures can be stranded in acquired characteristics which they don't know how to renounce after such a critical change. But there was always something beyond that in the Anacaon problem. Their grotesquely garish humanity served only to accentuate the fact that they were very alien.

They talked a lot, about themselves, about the *Zodiac* people, about recent history and about problems. They were easier with us than were the people of the *Zodiac*, because it did not mean so much that we were outworlders. Eve and I were less alien to the Anacaona than we were to Commander Hawke and Linda

Petrosian.

For the three younger people Micheal, naturally enough, was spokesman. Danel had little enough to say and offered hardly any comments for translation. Mercede was a little more forth-coming, but was largely content to echo and agree with the younger of her brothers.

I liked Micheal. He was shorter than Danel, but still a good deal taller than me. He was an intelligent man—or youth, as he seemed to be in Anacaon terms—but he seemed to have some difficulty in defining himself. He could talk about external events and things, but not about what he himself did or wanted to do.

He was curious about the star-worlds, and he prevailed on me to talk a little more than I would have liked about my own past. I hated descending to the level of traveller's tales and anec-dotes of long-lost experiences, but the questions forced a lot of conversation out of me. For this reason, I paid far less attention to the progress of the evening than I would have if I had found any direct opportunity to learn something.

As it was, the whole content of the night proved instantly forgettable apart from the tenuous impressions I've already mentioned.

It was very late when we finally got to bed. I didn't sleep immediately—my daily rhythm was probably more adaptable than Eve's, but even so Circadian rhythms can't be chopped and changed arbitrarily. I wasn't tired, and that was that. I swapped a few idle observations with the wind.

I wish I could sleep now, I said. I'm damn sure I won't be able to sleep easy out in the forest with no gun and no caller.

Coward, he said. It was a joke.

Perhaps I could lift a gun, I said pensively.

No chance, he predicted. I was inclined to agree with this assessment. The *Zodiac*s were playing the game seriously. Nobody was going to leave anything lying around.

Danel's probably reliable, the wind reassured me. And you know that jungles aren't dripping with danger Tarzan-style.

Nothing ever happens in the jungle.

People get ill, I said. Also there are insects. The little things are always far more bothersome than the big boys. And we don't even have our own medical kit.

Well...he said.

Well what? I demanded. What don't I want to hear this time?

I can cure insect bites, discourage leeches and keep you free from all parasitic infections, ecto- and endo-, he said.

You and Doc Miracle's Wonder Drug both, I commented drily.

Never say I didn't offer, he said.

I won't, I promised. And you're on. I've given up throwing fits. If you can pull enough tricks with my autonomic nervous system to keep me healthy, go ahead. Boost the talents of my bloodstream all you want. You have official permission to keep me in good health. Hell, why not? You're doing it anyway, aren't you? I do realise that I haven't had so much as a cold in the head since Lapthorn's Grave, and my staying power is better than it has any right to be at my age. So never say that I was ungrateful, okay?

I don't expect you to be grateful, he said. I know you don't like it. I know how attached you are to your own body. I wouldn't do anything you wouldn't do if you could, believe me.

I think I do, I said, generously.

The tone of the monologue is correct in suggesting that I had lost tension since we had last argued this particular point. The usefulness of the wind was beginning to be exploited. We were becoming more one than two. I could still call my body my own, but I had to credit certain aspects of its performance to the wind. At one time I had considered this to be an all-out assault on my individuality, but I was coming round to a different point of view. We could be two-in-one. We could be an individual together.

Maybe it doesn't make theoretical sense. But it made practical sense.

How are you with two-ton spiders? I asked him, on a whimsical last note before seeking the swathes of sleep.

Can't stand them, he said. Furry spiders are nice when they're little, but they shouldn't ever be allowed to grow up.

He claimed he hadn't got a sense of humour.

CHAPTER EIGHT

It was Max who gave me the full story as regards the crypto-arachnids (otherwise known as spiders).

Evolution on Chao Phrya had elected to tread pretty much the same boring path as on Earth and a whole host of other worlds, but slight differences in timing and anatomical organisation had resulted in big differences in the later stages. A million years or so isn't much in evolutionary terms, but that doesn't mean to say that a group can give the rest of creation that much start and still have no trouble in establishing itself at the level it could otherwise have attained.

What had happened on Chao Phrya was that the endoskeletal forms had been slow in coming out of the sea, and the exoskeletal forms had a good start on them in the matter of adapting to land life. The exoskeletals had used that time to solve all the problems which had proved crucial limitations on Earth: a clumsy breathing apparatus, an inefficient egg, and a brain built around the gullet.

On Earth and most other places it was the hardcored individuals who developed the cleidoic egg and—later—homoiothermy. On Chao Phrya the soft-cores beat them to it, so that when the exoskeletals finally emerged from the oceanic womb as air-breathers they met much tougher competition than statistical evidence suggested that they had any right to expect. The selective pressure on the hard-cores had soon pulled back the million years, but selective pressure works both ways, and they had never managed to dislodge the crypto-arthropods from the niches at the top of the Eltonian pyramid. The crypto-chordates supplied most of the herbivores, a lot of the insectivores, and the omnivorous Anacaona, but the crypto-arachnids and the crypto-scorpioids survived and thrived. Birds never got off the ground, and the soft-cores retained their monopoly on flying, but the types of tree available on Chao Phrya didn't offer much incentive to passeriformes, so perhaps that wasn't too surprising.

I couldn't help thinking that it would have been nice if the crypto-arthropods had managed some sentients, as they had contrived to dodge the hole-in-the-brain trap which had bugged the whole line on Earth. The galaxy is radically short of unchordate sentients. But even on Chao Phrya, the creepy-crawlies just didn't have it in them.

Pity.

Max delighted in showing off his knowledge of the science of life. His evolutionary account was a little doctrinaire, but he could afford to be proud of the way the *Zodiac* mob had buckled down to the task of getting to know their Promised Land. He was a bit free with words like 'impossible' and 'inevitable', and if he'd been some of the places I'd been he might well have modified his way of thinking. But I couldn't really blame him for having a narrow mind. He hadn't had much chance to broaden it.

My first impressions of the rain forest were distinctly unfavourable. It was, as I had prophesied, dark. But it wasn't quite the way I'd expected to find it. I'd not really been able to visualise just how high and dense the canopy would be.

We didn't have to hack our way through a glorified hawthorn hedge decked out with bindweed, thank heaven. We could walk without overmuch difficulty, although much of the time we were thigh-deep—sometimes waist-deep—in mushy fungus and other primitive plants.

The trees were gigantic—their trunks were thirty to fifty feet in diameter at chest height, and root tangles often doubled that close to the ground. The most dangerous impediment to our progress were root-ridges hidden by the clustering undergrowth. The canopy was the best part of a quarter of a mile up in the air. The branches were long, and much burlier than the whiplash-things we'd seen in the open country, but they were still flexible. They supported vast filamentous webs and whole decks of translucent membranes for extracting energy from the sunlight. The canopy wasn't deep, so far as I could judge, but it was very complicated. From on top, the forest had been green. From underneath, by transmitted instead of reflected light, it was bluey violet. The red wavelengths had been almost entirely filtered out, which implied that the photon traps in the lattice-work were of a very high order of sophistication and efficiency indeed.

The cover provided by the canopy was virtually total. There were no holes—only slightly brighter patches. The roof of the forest was a very efficient moisture trap. It was also a great big greenhouse. If it hadn't been for the fact that the trees used up most of the IR and deflected the rest, we would have been cooked. As it was we could have been a damn sight more comfortable. I judged that a lot of the nonphotosynthetic material in the ground cover was thermosynthetic rather than saprophytic. They took up a lot of the moisture, too, so that the humidity was only mildly unbearable.

The air in the forest was heady as well as damp. The oxygen content was a good eight to ten percent up on the open-land atmosphere, owing to the fact that the canopy discharged a lot of its waste gases down instead of up, and diffusion through the canopy was far too slow to compensate, at least during the day. At night the oxygen percentage declined slowly while the trees breathed but didn't photosynthesise.

As we progressed from the edge of the jungle, we grew progressively more intoxicated. It took several hours before our lungs adjusted and our brains acclimatised. We marched in single file. Danel and Mercede led, then Max, Eve, myself and Linda, with Micheal bringing up the rear.

'Nice, isn't it?' I said to Eve. She wasn't impressed. This was slightly odd—I hadn't quite expected her discomfort to cancel out her sense of wonder. Lapthorn's spirits had never been quelled by a little heat and moisture. Perhaps she wasn't quite as space-hungry as she thought she was. It had often struck me that she might be pushing herself too hard because of what had happened to her brother.

'Why isn't it green?' she asked.

I explained to her the difference between transmitted light and reflected light. She'd never encountered transparent foliage before. She looked annoyed when I explained. She'd known all along, really.

'It looks like one continuous sheet,' she complained. 'There's no real light getting in anywhere'

'The trees are separate, all right,' I assured her, 'but they have a beautiful gentleman's agreement about the space between the crowns. They can't overlap for more than a few inches, or we'd see the fringes. In any case, they have to bow their heads when it rains to make way for the water, and they couldn't do that if there was any substantial interlocking.'

'How does the excess water get out again?' she asked.

'Rivers,' I said briefly. Also, no doubt, evaporation from the canopy must be pretty terrific, since the laminae didn't have wax coats like the leaves of jungle trees on most worlds. But I didn't think it was worth complicating the discussion with a diatribe on water relations in subtropical environments.

'Actually,' Linda intervened, 'the canopy gets badly ripped during heavy rain, and the crowns fold up in order to regenerate. There's free evaporation then.'

I thanked her kindly for the supplemental information. Everybody on Chao Phrya seemed to know how the world worked. Knowledge is pride. Vanity is knowing more than you need to. Promised Land breeds vanity.

'Damn stuff is hell to clear,' supplied Max, referring more to the root formations than to the trees themselves. 'Can't drive proper roads through the forest. We wouldn't want to chop the trees down, of course, except so far as is necessary. But without roads the whole damn jungle is an impassable barrier.'

'Tough,' I commented unsympathetically. But I knew they'd find a way to bring civilisation to the land on the other side. They weren't the type of people to let a little tiny rain forest stand in the way of their ambition.

'We're not likely to encounter heavy rain, are we?' asked Eve of Linda.

'No,' Linda replied. 'Out of season. Everything is stable at this time of year.'

'I haven't seen any large animals yet,' said Eve.

'Lucky you,' I commented. 'Be content with all the crawlers in the undergrowth. They can prove troublesome enough in the long run, without our running into any giant spiders.'

'The bugs on the ground are safe,' said Max, dropping back so that he could address himself to me more easily. 'There are a lot of them, but none of them are likely to bite us. We don't taste that good. Provided that you don't mind sharing your boots with a few of them they won't bother you at all.'

'I believe you,' I said. 'But I'd still feel better with the medical resources of the *Swan* in my packsack. I don't trust that witch-doctor kit you've got. Don't you know that science has progressed while your granddaddies were locked up in their iron coffin?'

'We have everything we could possibly need,' said Linda, with a hint of petulance.

'You'd better be right,' I said, with fake ominousness.

'What about the Anacaona?' asked Eve. It was a good point. We had the best boots that the galaxy could supply, but we weren't vulnerable to the local bloodsuckers. They had light sandals, and they were.

'They'll be all right,' Max assured us. It was his best line. It seemed to be his only line. I'd have appreciated it far more if he'd occasionally tempered it with some kind of awareness of some of the things which could go wrong if they wanted to. He was too bloody cocky by half. I knew full well that nothing is ever as safe as he was assuring us that everything was.

I was always expecting something to go wrong, all the time

that I was hoping it wouldn't.

He must have sensed my distrust, because he laughed, and said: 'There's absolutely nothing here that can hurt you except for spiders and magna-drivers. The forest ecology is too straightforward to support more varied dangers than that. Everything else is only interested in plants and bugs.'

'And what,' I asked him, in tones suggesting weary suspicion, 'is a magna-driver?'

'About that big,' he said, measuring off two feet by one with his hands. 'The little bastards swarm in this stuff'—here he kicked up a mess of fungus and assorted vegetable debris with the toecap of his boot—'and creep up on the croppers. They can strip a whole herd to the bones in a matter of hours. A piteous sight. But they're not too strong. They're brittle and they're very vulnerable to a good bit of kicking. And they run like hell if you start to burn the ground cover.' He really relished the account.

'Don't you think,' I said patiently, 'that it would have been a good idea to mention such less than innocuous creatures *before* we actually got started?'

'Want to go back?' he asked.

'You know we can't go back,' I said. 'That's exactly why it's such a bloody good idea that you warn us about all these things before we start treading on them. Why the hell didn't you tell us last night?'

'Wasn't with you last night,' he pointed out. 'And I'm telling you now.'

'Oh God,' I said. 'You're a fool.'

'Thanks,' he said, unworried by the prospect.

'You've never been here before, have you?'

'Only briefly,' he said. 'Linda has.'

'With the Anacaona.'

'Of course.'

'Who know this place better than you could ever hope to know it. Doesn't it strike you as a considerable idiocy to march in here, knowing next to nothing about the practicalities of jungle expeditions, as if...' I paused '...as if you *owned* the bloody place.'

I should, of course, have realised before I began.

'Oh, the hell with the lot of you,' I said, with feeling. 'Give me that gun.'

'No.'

'Look,' I said, adopting the wrong approach as a matter of course, 'you aren't fit to be trusted with a bucket and spade. Give me the gun.'

'Go to hell,' he said.

I shook my head in tired despair. 'We very probably will,' I said. 'All of us. And sooner than you think.'

Which dire prediction closed the conversation.

I could count two things on my side—experience and the wind. Apart from those, I would have to place my meagre faith in the Anacaona and blind chance. What I didn't know about what could go wrong would have filled an encyclopaedia. I only hoped that Danel's years as a spiderhunter had given him all the expertise he needed. Somehow, I doubted it. He wasn't that old. I wondered how many spiders he had chopped to death with his trusty axe. He, at least, was appreciative enough of danger to carry a beamer to back him up in the event of unforeseen circumstance.

I couldn't relax.

I was concerned for Eve even more than for myself. She hadn't done anything to deserve this. She was going to be more uncomfortable than I. She was going to get a lot more tired than I. And she was in quasi-blissful ignorance of how bad it all was, which might keep her from being scared, but sure as hell wouldn't keep her from being careless. If anyone was fated to die on this crazy joyride, she was the number one candidate. I didn't like that. My life had already been sufficiently plagued by dying Lapthorns.

I found the excess of fellow-feeling an embarrassment.

We walked all day, and we sat still all night. So much for optimism.

When it began to get dark—and darkness in the forest was

as black as the caves of Rhapsody—we lit lamps and set about industriously clearing a space to pitch our tents in. The clearing was easy, because the plants which made up the bulk of the undergrowth were soft-structured and not attached to their roots with any degree of intimacy. For the first time, however, we were able to appreciate the multitudinous size of the creepy-crawly population. Though the insects here could grow as big as they wanted, most of them obviously found it convenient to stay small. The bugs looked offensively like bugs everywhere else. Shake a bush on virtually every populous world in the known galaxy, and the living detritus which falls to the ground will look pretty much the same. I've known bugs awaken quite a sense of nostalgia in some spacemen on worlds where every-thing else was noticeably unearthly. Not me, of course.

The kindly authorities who had been prevailed upon to supply our little expedition had seen fit to supply only three tents. We were obviously going to be crowded. Somewhat against my will, I was persuaded to share with Max.

The one good thing about our source of supply was that they didn't make us eat gruel. This was one advantage to their being so wilfully primitive. They just didn't realise how unusual it was for us to go such a long time without encountering either gruel or masquerading synthetics.

After supper, Max called up the base we'd left that morning and chatted amiably to the people who were theoretically looking after us. We didn't need a drop so soon, of course, but Max let them fix our beep so that they knew where we were. Just in case. I was surprised by this hint of caution—although it would have been matter-of-course under slightly different circumstances.

I wondered how much information about our progress was being reported back to Titus Charlot at the port. If any. It also occurred to me to wonder whether Charlot and Johnny were being cut in to the local superabundance of real food, or whether they were forced to eat out of ship's supplies. I would still have been happy to swap places with either one of them.

CHAPTER NINE

THE NEXT DAY WAS A carbon copy of the first except that we were all very stiff. We'd walked for over eight hours on the first day (real hours, not local) with only a couple of short breaks for rest and food to tide us over to supper. None of us was fit enough not to feel that kind of exertion. The wind undoubtedly helped to take a lot of the bite out of my stiffness, but I was still aware of my limbs and their protests. I could well imagine that the others—especially Eve—were really feeling themselves. Eve wouldn't complain, of course, and Max wouldn't even admit it. But Linda, though she was probably fittest of the three, wasn't ashamed to confess discomfort.

We'd all been spending too much time in trains and hover-crafts. Not to mention cars, beds and spaceships.

The Anacaona, however, were stepping just as sprightly as they had the previous day, and they seemed to be easily capable of coping with what was asked of them. But their limbs were naturally a good deal more flexible anyhow. They were probably equipped with far better natural shock and strain absorbers. The joys of a nomadic heritage.

Danel still led the way, plugging on with such a fierce and determined tread that those of us with shorter legs—all of us—were forced to call him back occasionally or ask him to pause while we caught up. We could hardly break into a canter while we were wading through sticky vegetation all the time.

I suspected that Danel was deliberately exploiting his own toughness to make us aware of our relative inadequacies.

Showing off, in short.

Danel was a strange person. As he was an alien, it stood to reason that I was going to find him strange, but he was an apparent oddity even when compared to his companions. There seemed to be something significant in his total withdrawal from us. The fact that he didn't speak English wasn't quite adequate to explain his lack of attempt to communicate. He never spoke to Linda, though she had a working knowledge of his tongue. Nor did he pass on remarks via Micheal or Mercede. His answers to relayed questions were always sharp and strictly to the point. He just didn't want to know about us. And yet he was our guide—his brother and sister were just along for the ride. His attitude seemed to me to be one of dumb hostility—passive protest. But Linda evidently took it for granted that he was guiding us conscientiously and competently. I decided eventually that he was trying to make evident some kind of contempt for humanity, in his own chosen fashion.

I didn't like to talk about the Anacaona to Linda while they were in earshot, and I'd missed my opportunity to get comprehensive information about them while we were *en route* from the capital. The best immediately available source of information was obviously Micheal, so I dropped back in line to join him, letting Eve and Mercede bunch up in front of me while Linda walked with Max some distance behind the big-striding Danel.

Micheal carried a larger pack than either Mercede or Danel. He seemed to be having no difficulty with it, but the distribution of labour seemed odd to me.

'You've got a lot of weight there to be carrying all day,' I said, to open conversation.

'It's no trouble,' he said.

'Is this how you usually travel?' I asked him. 'When you come out here hunting, with Danel?'

'Yes,' he said. 'Danel likes to be able to move very quickly.'

'The spiders are that dangerous, then?' I probed.

'Not really,' he said. 'But we seek them out rather than

avoiding them.'

'What exactly do you hunt spiders for?' I asked him. 'What good are they?'

'No good at all,' he replied. 'We use them—for clothes, sometimes to make other things. Sometimes to eat. But there is nothing we can get from the spiders that the people of the *Zodiac* cannot give us.'

'And you'd rather use the stuff from the *Zodiac* than get your own?'

'It's better,' he said.

'But Danel hunts spiders,' I said. 'He wears that breastplate thing, which is presumably spider hide, or spider shell, or whatever you call it.'

'Danel likes to hunt spiders,' Micheal explained.

'Danel doesn't like the people of the *Zodiac*?'

'Perhaps not.'

I observed the diplomatic 'perhaps.'

'And you like to hunt with him,' I said amiably. 'And carry the bulk of the load. And you don't even carry a gun to protect yourself.'

'Danel needs someone to hunt with him,' said Micheal flatly, as though that were the sum total of the explanation.

'Rather you than me,' I said drily, though it was an extremely pointless remark. I was eyeing his pack and estimating how much heavier than mine it was. He was a strong man. My capabilities, though, had declined since the days before Lapthorn's Grave. Even with the help of the wind I wasn't able to make quite as much use of myself. My semi-fascination with the size of Micheal's load was only a reflection of my own realisation of my decline. Age had rubbed a bit of my capability right out. Two years on that black mountain had reversed the direction of my life's progress. If I didn't fight tooth and claw to retain myself, my days as a crack pilot would be over in seven years and I'd have to take up engineering or liner-jockeying or renew a long-abandoned intimacy with the ground. The two years which I owed Charlot might be two of the last of my best, and that wasn't going to make them pass any faster or any easier. Lapthorn's Grave had set me on the downhill ride.

But that wasn't what I wanted to talk to Micheal about, and I cleared my mind of it. I talked a little about the forest, but as soon as I managed to actually involve him in the conversation, we had to talk a little more about me. He was interested in me. I told him a few irrelevancies about my personal history and my way of life. Finally, I gained the confidence to touch on certain subjects which might have proved offensive if introduced without care.

'That spiel you were pouring out night before last,' I said. 'It was mostly for show, wasn't it?'

'Spiel?' he queried.

'Sorry,' I said. 'The conversation we all had in your house. It was an exhibition, wasn't it? It was faked.' It wasn't a very friendly thing to say, but I thought that the Anacaon conception of good manners paid a lot more respect to the truth than ours does.

'Why do you say that?' he asked. I glanced ahead. Linda was too far ahead to overhear, and Eve and Mercede weren't listening.

'It was a show for Linda,'' I said. 'For the people of the *Zodiac*. You've never said a word on your own behalf, have you? Your whole dealings with the humans are conditioned by what the humans want from you, aren't they?'

'Of course,' he said. I wondered just how inevitable that was. Attitude is always affected by what people expect, but the Anacaona seemed to have adapted with remarkable enthusiasm and facility to their human-defined role in the Promised Land. It didn't seem natural to me.

'Why do you capitulate to such an extent so easily?' I asked him directly.

'I can't answer that,' he said. 'It's a question that I can only define in your terms, and in those terms it's a question which doesn't need to be asked.'

'I don't see that,' I said.

'It's a human question,' he said. 'I can only give a human answer. And once I can give a human answer, the question is already settled. There can't be a reason, in your terms, and the reason in our terms can't be put into human terms.'

I tried to follow all that.

'What you're saying,' I decided finally, 'is that in order to communicate with the people of the *Zodiac*, you've found it necessary to develop a personality with which they *can* communicate, because they *couldn't* communicate with you as you are. The basis you've established for communication has been almost exclusively dictated by their angle of the communication, right?'

'I think so.'

'And Danel won't communicate because he doesn't want his mind polluted.'

'No. Not at all. Danel does not communicate directly. He has not acquired many human attributes. The relationship between these two things is not deliberate.'

I tried to follow *that*. I tried to estimate its importance, and couldn't quite manage it. What Micheal was telling me was that the Anacaon mind was so alien that in order to communicate with the people of the *Zodiac*, they had had to manufacture a human mentality. Danel had not manufactured such a mentality. But could he avoid being affected, if all his own people were so busy being human? How could a mind so alien as the Anacaon mind have such a facility for co-adaptation to the human mind? *Why* did it have such a facility?

Micheal wasn't talking to me as a member of an alien race. He was talking to me as a part of the Promised Land.

Instant humanity. Just add...what?

'You could have killed them all,' I said. 'You still could. Sheer force of numbers. Wipe them out. Your people didn't have to be enslaved. They could have reacted, and remained themselves.'

'Why?' he asked.

Why indeed? It wasn't a question. He didn't mean 'Why?' at all. He meant that I was off the track again. He couldn't answer except in human terms, and once he had human terms to answer with, the question became redundant. There was a communication block between us. I could only talk to the human in him, but I wanted to talk to the Anacaon.

'Don't you find it a hell of a way to be?' I asked him. 'Doesn't it offend you, having to be what someone else says you must be?'

'No,' he said. Which struck me as being very odd. If his identity was willing to be moulded so easily, how come he had an identity in the first place? And how was I supposed to explain Danel?

'What about Danel?' I asked.

'It's the same,' he said, with a shrug of his shoulders. A very human shrug.

For a minute or two, I didn't understand. Then inspiration struck.

'It's a different role in the same play,' I said. 'He's Linda Petrosian's alien. An ersatz noble savage. You're all too good to be true, so....'

It was a deceptively simple thought. The Anacaona had a very highly developed talent for mimicry. But how come? What could it possibly have been used for before the *Zodiac* landed? How could it have evolved? And what was it for? Moths pretend to be dead leaves or vile-tasting cousins so that they won't get eaten by predators. Praying mantises pretend to be twigs for precisely the reverse reason. But neither could be applicable to the Anacaona by any stretch of the imagination.

The idea of a race living behind masks for the benefit of other races wasn't new to me. Colonised planets often result in that sort of effect. Humans are notoriously intolerant people, and the rule on a lot of worlds is 'pretend, or suffer,' no matter what the Law of New Rome may have to say on the subject. But the Anacaona were a step beyond that. The other races wore their masks obviously. Their resentment was often an integral part of the mask. But the *Zodiac* people obviously trusted the Anacaona implicitly and that trust had never been betrayed.

Was there any Anacaon left behind Micheal's mask? Was there even any behind Danel's?

Micheal was impressively bland about the whole thing. I continued to ask him leading questions. I tried to be devious, and employed a few trick questions to try and reach something in him that was beyond his fake, frail humanity. But he was open and apparently honest, and he knew what I was asking him, and there was no help he could give me. To all the most awkward questions, his blanket answer was that in human terms they were redundant, in other terms meaningless.

It occurred to me then that if Charlot was having acute difficulties with the Anacaona in the colony, then my feeble mind had no chance at all to sort out the mystery.

I was sure that Micheal was telling me the truth, but I was also fairly sure that it was a special kind of truth. I had to be content in the meantime with wary ignorance. Perhaps I would never get beyond that.

'Is the colony on New Alexandria a success?' asked Micheal.

'I don't know much about it,' I told him. 'I only found out about it a few weeks ago—indirectly. But I guess it can't be an unqualified success if people are running away from it. You can hardly pass off a kidnap as behaviour expected of the colonists. The woman who escaped with the child must have had reasons, and I can't see that they would be human reasons.'

'What is a kidnap?' asked Micheal.

That gave me pause to think.

'The stealing of one person by another,' I told him. It didn't sound to me like the Anacaon style at all. I had suspected that Charlot wasn't telling us all he knew, and might be deceiving us to some extent, but I hadn't really thought that he might be spinning us a complete lie. He had been insistent enough about the kidnapping to make it look very definite indeed. And his expectation of New Rome backing was obviously real.

'What do you think about that possibility?' I asked Micheal. 'Why would an Anacaon do something like that?'

'No Anacaon would.'

'But it did happen,' I said. 'Believe me, Titus Charlot isn't the sort of man who runs prisons. And why should he, with a people as co-operative as yours. I suppose it's possible that the girl went with the woman of her own free will, but why would they leave New Alexandria illegally? Why would they want to leave?'

'Ask the *Zodiac* people whether any Anacaon has ever committed a crime of any kind,' suggested Micheal.

'I don't have to,' I said. 'I accept your assurance, believe me. So the Anacaona aren't very human at all. Committing crimes is virtually universal among humans.'

'We aren't human,' he assured me. And, of course, that was true. The Anacaona were in no way human beings. They were merely living up to human expectations. Moths don't become dead leaves. They remain moths. But they live up to all the eye's expectations of a dead leaf. Until they fly away. Was what the woman had done the single Anacaon action that I had been searching for? If so, what had inspired it? What could possibly have overridden the adaptive compulsion?

I decided that it *had* to be a compulsion. I couldn't imagine a whole race whose dearest wish was to be the perfect slave race. I looked forward to meeting the 'wild' Anacaona. Perhaps that would reveal something.

'What do you think might have happened on New Alexandria?' I asked him. 'Can you think of any chain of circumstance which could present us with our present situation?'

'I can't think of anything,' he said. 'But there is a rumour.'

'What rumour?' I demanded. I really felt that I should have been let in on this previously. Surely Max or Linda would have told me if they had known.

'The girl was an Indris,' said Micheal. 'That's only a rumour.'

'What's an Indris?' I inquired politely.

'I think you'd call it an idol,' he said.

'A god?' I asked, sorely puzzled.

'Not a real god,' he said. 'A false one.'

'The girl was a false god,' I repeated; just to be sure I'd got it right. 'What does that mean? I mean, does that provide an explanation for the woman's behaviour?'

'I don't know,' he said. Having casually let slip his revelation about what the grapevine was saying, he now couldn't see any significance to it at all.

I'd been doing far too much thinking. I gave up.

The tail end of the conversation cast doubts on all my earlier conclusions and speculations. I was no longer sure that I'd inferred correctly what he was trying to tell me. I realised that I utterly and completely failed to understand, and that I'd have to be content with that until I got another blinding flash of inspiration. Perhaps I never would. There are, it is said, certain alien races which are completely beyond human understanding. That was almost inevitable. We have limited minds. But it was a provocative thought that a species could be beyond human understanding while we were apparently well within the scope of theirs. Especially when said species was at a very primitive level indeed. What, I wondered, did that imply?

It was all too much for me to flog my mind about at the time. I gave it a rest, and was content to kick plants to pieces and study the vast tree trunks for a while. It occurred to me that I couldn't see the wood for the trees. I was too close to it all. I would have been very grateful for an incisive dialogue with Charlot to clear up my confusion.

After we'd eaten, and compensated somewhat for the gap in our stomachs, I decided to have a round of conversation with Linda, to find out exactly how much she didn't know.

'What's the crime rate among the Anacaona?' I asked her.

'There's no crime,' she said. 'The Anacaona are an honest people.'

'Even when they're abused?'

'They're not.'

'They were.'

'There were no crimes. No trouble at all.'

'How do you explain that?'

'It doesn't need an explanation. It's a fact. Crimes need

explaining, not the absence of them.'

That seemed to me to be a negative point of view, and a convenient justification of ignorance, but I didn't bother to say so.

'What's an Indris?' I asked, instead.

'An Anacaon myth.'

'Do the Anacaona have a complicated mythology?'

'The wild ones do, yes. The Anacaona who have been associated with the *Zodiac* have lost virtually all traces of it, though. Either that or they disseminate it strictly in private.'

That struck me as being a very odd point of uncertainty for someone who claimed to be an alien anthropologist. It suggested that Linda Petrosian's failure to understand the Anacaona might be as absolute as my own. She trusted their actions implicitly, but retained doubts about their inmost thoughts.

'What's the Indris myth?' I asked her.

'Indris is a plural and singular name. It was borrowed from our language as a label to apply to an individual or a group of people or things which used to be worshipped.'

'Used to be?'

'The Indris used to be alive, in legend. They are now thought of as having been extinct for a long time. They are now thought of as having been false gods.'

'Is that your doing?'

'No. The Anacaona have believed the Indris to be false gods for a long time now.'

'What have they replaced them with?'

'Nothing.'

'Nothing?' It didn't seem likely that a race should declare one set of gods false without finding some truer ones. Not at the primitive level, anyhow.

'The Anacaona seem to be quite free of superstition now.'

I pondered for a few moments. 'Are you sure,' I said slowly, 'that there was ever a time when the Anacaona thought that the Indris were *real* gods?'

'Of course,' she said. 'It wouldn't make sense for them to

have gods which they knew to be false, would it?'

I supposed not.

'Micheal told you about the Indris, didn't he?' she asked.

'Did you know about this rumour?' I asked her.

'Yes.'

'But you didn't think it was worth mentioning to us?'

'No. It's ridiculous.'

'Well, who started it and what keeps it in circulation?'

'I don't know.'

'Thanks a lot.'

'If I'd thought it was important,' she said, 'I'd have told you. But I didn't. I don't know anything about it, and it doesn't make sense. If it originates with the wild Anacaona, I can't imagine how they could have got hold of such an idea, unless your woman told them.'

'She's not my woman,' I said stiffly. 'And I can't think of any conceivable reason why she should say such a thing...Except one,' I added.

'What's that?' she asked.

'It might be true,' I said.

CHAPTER TEN

THERE WAS A CERTAIN amount of friction between Max and Danel. It was not that Danel was uncooperative—like all the Anacaona, Danel was the soul of co-operation—nor that Max was over-exhibiting his dislike for the Anacaona. It was simply a clash of roles. Insofar as it was a war at all, it was a cold and bloodless one.

In my opinion, Danel cast a slight shadow on the picture Micheal had inspired in me of the Anacaona as the perfect people to share a planet with. I wished that I could talk to him, or to Mercede, because I had a feeling that they might put the whole story in a different light.

But I could only talk about Danel to Micheal, to Linda, and to Max. When we were in the tent that evening, Max and I had a quiet drink before bedtime. I felt that it was some measure of acceptance that he offered me a share of his private supply of booze. Perhaps he was relenting. It didn't endear him to me greatly, though. Not much.

'You don't get on with Danel, do you?' I said. I wasn't enamoured of Max's line in private chit-chat, so I thought I might as well come straight to the points which interested me.

'I don't like him,' said Max.

'Why not?'

'Because he makes a big thing out of being a big guy. He kills spiders with his axe just for the fun of it, and sets his little brother up to play tunes for them while he does it. He makes a big thing about being at home in the forest and I'm damned if he knows the place any better than I do. He isn't wild, no matter how much he pretends. He's a fake.'

'Strikes me that ought to offend Linda more than it bugs you,' I said. 'I thought she was the one who was deeply into sharing the planet with the Anacaona. I thought you wanted to leave them alone to do whatever they want.'

'You're on a different wavelength, Grainger,' he told me. 'I don't give a damn about goldens in general. I don't think we have to look after them because they're part and parcel of our beloved planet. I don't give a damn about anything that doesn't touch me. But Danel touches me. Here and now. If he's going to help us, he should help us and forget this bloody no-speak pantomime.'

'You don't care about why he is that way?'

'No. Don't get me wrong, I don't have anything against goldens. Just because I turned down their invitation to supper the other night doesn't mean to say I can't stand to set foot in their homes. It's just that I don't like this whole farce about who does what when. They're all too bloody nice or too bloody distant. They're a bunch of hypocrites and that's all there is to it. They're harmless, and they're useful, but don't let anyone ever tell you that they're God's gift to the *Zodiac*. Because they're not. Whatever they do it's for their own reasons—I don't know what they are or what the hell, but I sure as hell know they weren't created purely and simply for our convenience and amusement, which is what Linda and her gang seem to think. It has nothing to do with the Promised Land argument—that's a tired argument anyway—it's just that because they're so helpful and live up to all our expectations that people like Linda feel they've got to like the bastards. Well, not me. I'm not going out of my way to hate them, but when I'm standing next to them I'll be damned if I'll love one just because he's got cute notions about the old days and the old ways. See?'

'I see,' I said. 'But you're making no effort to understand.'

'Hell,' he said, 'if I tried to understand everything in this life I'd go crazy. Do you understand us, let alone them?'

'I can rationalise human behaviour,' I told him.

'Nuts,' he said. 'You don't understand, and damn your rationalising human behaviour. There's a hell of a lot in life that I'll never understand and it won't hurt me in the least. Why bother? Do what you do, and damn reducing it all to clockwork.'

It was a nice philosophy. All right, I guess, for those people who think like that. Lapthorn was always content to feel rather than to know. He demanded explanations, all right—he was as curious a man as I've ever encountered—but his explanations weren't the same as mine. I wanted to know why things happened. He only wanted to know how, and especially how it felt. Max wasn't even a Lapthorn. He was content, so far as I could see, just to go through it all. But perhaps that was a bad judgement. People are very rarely honest about themselves in that kind of account.

'If Danel is so bent on being untouched by human hands,' I said, 'why did he agree to guide us?'

'I'll give you three reasons,' he said generously. 'Personally, I don't believe in any of them. One: he was told to by someone, human or Anacaon. Two: he wants to show off his Anacaon pride and integrity to the full. Three: he thinks that the people you're trying to find might be worth a look on his own behalf. Okay?'

'Not really,' I said. 'The last one—you mean that you think the girl is an Indris.'

'He might.'

'You think he might be right?'

'Don't be a fool. Look, can't we drop this interrogation business, just for once? Anyone would think to listen to you that this whole farce is just a blind for a spying trip. I never knew anybody try to find out so much so fast. If we weren't miles from anywhere in a bloody jungle I'd swear you were picking up information for some undercover purpose.'

I was astounded by this accusation.

'Who the hell would want to spy on you?' I demanded.

'Come off it,' he said. 'I'm not a baby. We may be cut off here, and we may not want to know about your great big wonderful galaxy, but we have to know enough to look after our own interests. What about these people who go around buying and selling worlds? What about the people who move in to strip planets of all the ore they can get in the shortest possible time?'

I think he was talking about the Caradoc Company and its brethren. He had the right idea about their sharkish temperament and methodology, but he knew absolutely nothing about the feasibility of the sort of tactics he was talking about.

'Sure,' I said, 'the galaxy is full of nasty people like that. Worlds are worth money. But not worlds like this one. They're a dime a dozen. With people on, that is. Without people, they can be turned into very nice resorts by the experience-sellers. Experience goes over like a bomb these days. Not ore. Raw materials are easy to get hold of. Far too easy. What's worth money these days is something that can't be mined or mass-produced. Knowledge and heritage fetch big money through the New Alexandrian processing machine, but what the companies are more interested in is buying and selling war and paradise. They deal in big games on a big scale. They don't leave anything which will turn them a profit lying around, if they can help it, but I can assure you that they wouldn't pay a spy to look around down here. Your purple greenhouses aren't nearly nice enough. You don't grow any nice drugs. You just haven't anything they want, because you've already destroyed the potential paradise value of your planet by living on it. Besides which, you know full well that New Rome empowers itself to take all necessary steps to protect indigenes. Your planet has indigenes—the Anacaona.'

He didn't believe me. He really didn't believe me.

'You can't possibly think we're here under subterfuge?' I said.

He shrugged.

'Is that why your government is making things so bloody difficult?' I asked him. Then I thought for a moment and added: 'No. Can't be. No matter how paranoid your people are they'd accept the credentials of Titus Charlot and the Law of New Rome, wouldn't they?'

Still, it did go some way to explaining the bloodymindedness of the *Zodiac* people's whole attitude to the mission.

'Look,' said Max. 'I don't really care who you are. I got this job because somebody has to wet-nurse you two, no matter what your job is. If it makes you feel any better, I guess I don't think you're conspiring to take our planet away from us, but I wouldn't be surprised if some of the crew think exactly that. Paranoid is what some of them are, all right. The minute anyone starts threatening incidents and legal pressures and gunboats, the crew get very uptight, and who can blame them? But don't try to tell me that we aren't doing the right thing by you. We're helping you, like you asked, and we're doing all we can.

'Any case, what the hell do you think we care about some ship dumping a couple of goldens way out in the jungle? We don't—that's how much we care. What the hell did you expect us to do when you turned up bawling at us out of the sky? Roll out a red carpet and give you our entire police force plus Sherlock Holmes? This is a busy world, Grainger. We've got no unemployment here. We don't have to sell this experience you're talking about because we've got it. We're building this world. You were bloody lucky that the Commander spared a couple of people and let you play your silly games at all. The Anacaona will find your two. If you want them back the Anacaona will let us have them. I don't get this whole deal, but what I do know is that to us *it isn't that important.*

'So don't throw your weight about like the captain himself were back of you. You're nothing, Grainger.'

And that, as they say, was really telling me.

There was no point in starting a fight. These people were difficult to deal with because they were difficult to deal with, and that was that. This wasn't Rhapsody, where you could treat everyone like a lunatic. There really wasn't much point in my hammering away at everybody trying to get answers to questions they didn't consider worth asking.

I talked to the wind, instead. At least I could get some intelligent conversation there.

This is all getting distinctly tedious, I said.

You don't say, he replied. Whose fault is that? Take it easy. You'll be wandering around in this forest for a good many days yet. Enjoy the scenery. It's more fun that way.

Thank you for the suggestion. Do you have any light to shed on our various problems, though? Any helpful hints on how to understand this affair?

One extra question, he said.

Well come on, then, I said. Don't be shy.

We haven't seen anything which suggests that the Anacaona are the end product of an evolutionary chain. I know all the story Max gave you, and it's no doubt true as far as it goes. But the mammals here—or their conceptual equivalent—have never had the development they had back on good old Earth. Sure, there are these croppers—anything from rabbits to elephants, as I understand the colloquial usage of the term. But there are emphatically no monkeys. I don't believe that the Anacaona could possibly have evolved here. They're no more indigenous than the people of the *Zodiac*.

Marvellous, I commented.

It was a hypothesis well worth considering, of course, but it hardly made matters any simpler. If anything, it made for even more complications.

Roll on next week, I said, as I dropped off to sleep.

CHAPTER ELEVEN

THE NEXT DAY WAS another exceptionally heavy one for those of us who were less than fully tuned up—which was all of us except Danel. Even Micheal was beginning to show signs of stress.

Danel ploughed on with the same grim relentlessness. His feet came down hard, virtually splashing his way through the soft carpet of delicate plants. The ground was becoming more and more difficult. It was far from even, and the slopes we had to negotiate were made that much more treacherous by virtue of the fact that the vegetation crowded them and to some extent concealed their real topography. It was never possible now to pick our way around the worst of the ground cover—we had to plunge on through it whether it was ankle-deep or waist-deep. Luckily, Danel's purposeful stride took on the heaviest part of the burden of clearing a way. Max and I took it in turns to go second and make a further contribution to the comfort of those in the rear. On dropping back at one point to let Max take over, my tiredness seemed more than a little irksome because I could not see the point of Danel's insistent pace.

'Look,' I said to Micheal, 'he's got to slow down. We just can't move this fast as a party. Doesn't he know anything about the convoy principle? Somebody's going to come to grief soon if he doesn't stop forcing that furious pace.'

'I've told him,' said Micheal. 'I don't think he's listening. There's something on his mind.'

'Great,' I said. 'There's something on his mind. What about

Mercede? Can't she persuade him to stop? She's suffering as much as anyone except Eve.' Eve, of course, was worst affected by the implacability of the pace. We'd lightened her pack somewhat, but her feet were blistered and the blisters were bursting, and there was nothing we could do about that. If we'd had medicine from the *Swan* at least she could have had stimshots to stop her caring too much, but she wouldn't trust what was on offer from the *Zodiac* kit, and I didn't blame her.

'I don't think so,' said Micheal feebly. I realised belatedly that he was a little preoccupied himself.

Something was wrong.

'For God's sake tell me,' I said. 'What's he going so fast for?'

'He wants to reach the forest people as fast as possible.'

'Why?'

'Before he....' Micheal searched for the words.

'You mean he's sick,' I supplied.

'I think so,' he said.

'And you're sick too?'

'Yes.'

'Mercede?'

He shrugged uncomfortably. It was obvious that he thought they were all ill.

'What is it?'

'I don't know. Something we picked up in the jungle. These things are carried by parasites.'

'You can't all have been bitten by the same bug,' I said.

He shook his head. 'Once one of us was infected,' he said, 'sharing the same tent...with half a hundred insects....'

I looked ahead again, at Danel's distant figure. He didn't want to be ill while he was guiding us. If all three Anacaona fell ill, we would be on our own, and with a considerable burden besides. I cursed the fact that this would probably cost us more time, but most of all I cursed our luck. It wasn't their fault, when all was said and done. I was tempted to blame the *Zodiac* people and their parsimony in the matter of equipment, but there was no point in that either.

'Look,' I said to Micheal. 'Tell him not to kill himself. If we can't reach the forest people, we can't. This is doing no good at all.'

But the advice came far too late. Danel was out of sight as I spoke, and as I moved forward to go after him, Eve fell. I hesitated, then called to Max to stop Danel, and went back.

She had been frightened by a spider. Not a big one, by Chao Phryan standards, but a web-spinner as big as a football. She had almost stepped on it as it had tried to scuttle across her path, turned sideways and tripped over a root. She had hurt her shin and turned her ankle. It was nothing serious and wouldn't have delayed us for more than a few moments. But by the time those few moments were over, Micheal had sunk to the ground in what appeared to be a fit of utter exhaustion, and Max had come back to us to tell us that he had been unable to stop Danel. The spiderhunter was getting farther and farther ahead of us with every moment, and on the day's form so far he would neither notice nor care that we were no longer close behind him.

'We'd better stop,' I said.

Eve protested, but Max agreed with me. Micheal was conscious and apparently willing to go on, but he was in no fit condition. I could see no symptoms of any disease, but I hardly knew what to look for. Mercede was still apparently healthy.

Max directed Linda to make coffee and soup, while he began clearing a space where we could sit without being plagued by bugs.

'What sort of sickness is it?' I asked Micheal. 'Can you estimate how long it will last? Have you even any idea what effects it will have?'

But he didn't know. He wasn't a doctor. How was he supposed to know exactly what was wrong with him? Besides which, sicknesses varied in their effects. Sometimes people died, sometimes they dreamed aloud. By 'dreaming aloud' I suspected that he meant to indicate delirium. This implied that the sickness might have a fever stage, like most of the familiar jungle diseases on Earth, and those which could affect humans on other worlds.

'Have you got anything in that do-it-yourself witchdoctor kit that might help him?' I asked Max.

Max shook his head. 'Don't know anything about it,' he said. 'Can't really risk giving human medicine to a golden. After all, we don't catch the disease, so we can't really be expected to know anything about treating it.'

'How about you, expert?' I asked Linda, with a hint of exasperated malice in my voice.

'I don't know,' she said.

We had no alternative but to leave Micheal to Mercede, knowing that the girl was also ill and would probably not be able to help in a matter of hours.

'Perhaps it's as well that Danel keeps going,' said Eve. 'If he reaches the forest people he can probably get help.'

'And if he doesn't,' I said, 'he'll be on his own out there with no help at all for himself.'

There was an uncomfortable silence.

Nobody moved except Eve, who walked around and around in a tight circle, testing her creased ankle.

'Well now, captain,' I said, to rub a little of my spite off on to her, 'we seem to be in one hell of a mess now.'

She didn't react, so I looked elsewhere for a target for my asperity. But there was no point, and I soothed my bad nerves carefully.

'Better get on the blower to home,' I suggested to Max. 'Explain to them the geometry of the situation and tell them we need help. They can parachute somebody down through the canopy, can't they?'

'They could,' he said. He didn't seem to think they would.

'Tell them it's urgent,' I said. 'A matter of life and death.'

'I'll try,' he said.

But the people on the other end didn't seem to think that there was any effective help that they could render. They'd be pleased to drop supplies, but not doctors. They didn't have anyone who knew anything at all about Anacaon sicknesses and they didn't know anyone who did. Yes, of course they'd inquire among the Anacaona, but they weren't optimistic. They didn't think that the Anacaona treated diseases. Just rode them out or died. Max confirmed that this judgement was in accordance with his own knowledge of affairs, and so did Linda. Of course the Anacaona got sick. Everybody gets sick. But not everybody gets neurotic enough about it to try and cure the sick. Some people just take it as it comes and let it go if it will. That, apparently, was the Anacaon view of life.

'Bloody hell,' I said, with feeling. And we all sat down to wait for night.

Micheal played his panpipes all evening. Linda and I kept him company in one tent, while Mercede was persuaded to rest in the other, with Eve watching for any sign of her getting worse. Max, we supposed, was in the other tent.

We managed to locate a whole series of minute puncture wounds on the lower part of Micheal's legs. Apparently he was quite accustomed to sharing a little of his flesh with the forest creatures while he was out here. He probably didn't even notice the bites. We washed the wounds and put bandages around his calves, but it all felt completely futile. We dared not apply anything like antiseptics or bug-killing drugs. We had no idea what effect they might have within his metabolism. We waited, and we listened to his music.

The tune he played was plaintive and highly structured. His boneless fingers flowed over the surface of the pipes, constructing chains of cadences whose complexities were explored in all combinations and every last detail. It seemed to me to be very mathematical music, lacking in the touch of magic which I felt was necessary in aesthetic appeal. But I'm no music lover, and wiser men might have deemed it brilliant for all I could tell.

I just didn't like it.

Once, as he paused, I asked him how he felt. He couldn't tell me.

'There's nothing you can do,' he said. 'Except wait.'

'Would you rather Mercede was with you?' asked Linda.

'Better not,' he said. 'She might not have caught it.' He was fingering the pipes fluidly, and I could see that his attention was returning to them.

'The music you play,' I said. 'Do you remember it or do you make it up as you go along?'

He blew a couple of experimental notes.

'I make it up,' he said. 'That kind of song. There are some things that have to be remembered.'

'Like the music you play for the spiders?'

He shook his head weakly. 'Not necessarily,' be said. 'But that music has to be played right. It has to be built properly.'

He didn't want to talk any more. He began to play again, but quietly and absently, without the meticulous attention to order that had been implicit before. He roamed across the full range of the instrument. Linda and I simply listened.

Later, I said to him: 'Can you talk?' He had put the pipes away.

'What do you want me to talk about?' he asked.

'The Indris.'

He didn't seem inspired by the mention of the topic.

'False gods,' he said, in tired tones. 'But they were a great people.'

'Your ancestors?'

'Yes.'

'In what way were they different?'

'In many ways.'

'This girl. You say that she might be an Indris. It's rumoured, anyhow. I've seen her, and she looked exactly like an Anacaon to me. How would I know if she was an Indris?'

'You wouldn't,' he said, stressing the 'you' very slightly:

'But an Anacaon could tell?'

'Yes.'

'How?'

'The difference is in the thinking. In the language.'

'Your language?'

'Yes.'

'Your language inevitably reflects differences in thinking, then?'

'That's the way it's used.'

'That's why you never tell lies?'

'Yes.'

'But you don't tell lies in English, either.'

He smiled faintly. 'English is used in a different way,' he said. 'We never lie. But sometimes the language lies. It is the way things are said in the language.'

Linda took hold of my arm. 'Leave him alone, can't you?' she said. 'This isn't doing anyone any good.'

'It's doing *me* good,' I said. 'I'm beginning to understand why we can't understand or use their language. I'm beginning to understand why a child of English-speaking parents on New Alexandria was allowed to grow up speaking only her own language.'

'You don't think the girl could possibly be an Indris, do you?' she asked, incredulously.

'Maybe,' I said.

'But the Indris are a legend,' she protested.

'Micheal,' I said, to attract his attention again. His eyes were closed, but he was not asleep. He opened them, and looked at me somewhat reproachfully—or so I imagined.

'One more question,' I said. 'Did the Indris have spaceships? Did they travel between the stars?'

'Yes,' he said.

'It's not true,' said Linda Petrosian.

'The Anacaona don't lie,' I told her.

'He isn't lying. He believes it. But it's only a legend. It's a matter of faith, not historical truth.'

'Yet he calls them *false* gods,' I reminded her. 'He's not that credulous.'

'Remember what he said about the language lying,' she said, in a last desperate appeal to her brand of reason. 'The absurdity must be coming out of the translation. We don't really know what he's saying.'

'I know what he's saying,' I said.

'We'd have found traces,' she insisted. 'You can't possibly believe that a starfaring people came to this world, colonised it, and then abandoned their children to degeneracy and wiped out all traces of any civilisation.'

'That depends,' I mused, 'on when. When did they come here? Where did they go? It might have been millions of years ago. We've always assumed that the Gallacellans were the first. Then us. Then the Khor-monsa. All within the space of a few thousand years. No older race ever tried to colonise. They were all content to stay at home, like ninety-nine out of every hundred even today. But there's no reason to assume there haven't been a hundred or a thousand other interstellar cultures.'

'Where are they now?'

'That,' I told her, 'is an entirely different order of question.'

'You can't ignore it like that.'

'No more can you ignore the fact that the woman we're looking for has behaved in a way which is totally alien to your idea of the Anacaona. She's committed crimes. There must be a reason for that. There must be a reason why she came back here. There's something important involved here, and I'm not content to clear up this mess without finding out what it is. Perhaps you are. For a supposed expert on the Anacaona you're surprisingly content with your ignorance. But I care. I want to know what I'm doing. I tried to help that girl once, now I'm trying to do it again. I didn't know what was happening last time—this time I'm damned if I'll let it go without trying to find out. No one else here seems the least bit interested in what's happened to that girl. The Anacaona have absorbed a great deal of your culture and your thought and your way of doing things, but I think you've been affected by them, too. Not in an imitative way, but affected nevertheless. You're content to let things be so long as they work to your advantage. You couldn't understand them, and in the end they've led you to give up *trying* to understand. Not just them—everything. I guess the *Zodiac* generations gave your people a long head start in being small-minded, but you're sure as hell making no attempt to expand again. The only thing you want to grow is the quantity of sacred soil that you can plant your footprints on. I don't think I ever met two people who didn't give a damn about as much as you and Max.'

I guess Chao Phrya and its purple jungle must have been vaguely conducive to running off at the mouth. It was getting to be a habit, and not just with me. When the going gets rough I usually clam up tight and devote myself to looking after number one. But I was getting intellectual in my old age. I wondered whether it might not be me who was caring far too much about everything that went on around me.

'What are we going to do tomorrow?' asked Linda finally.

'I'm going on,' I told her. 'I have to. Eve will come with me, and maybe Max. If Danel returns, we'll go with him instead of with Max. If he's well, that is.'

'You'll have no interpreter,' she pointed out.

'We'll just have to get along without,' I said.

'You'd better get some sleep,' she advised.

I nodded, and stood to leave the tent. 'If anything happens,' I said, 'call me.'

I went out, sealing the flap behind me. I looked in on Eve and Mercede. Both were fast asleep.

The other tent was dark. I didn't want to stumble around in the dark, so I took a lantern in with me, expecting to find Max in his sleeping bag, dead to the world.

He wasn't.

He'd gone.

CHAPTER TWELVE

WHEN THE NEXT MORNING dawned, I checked with both tents. Micheal was worse. He was awake, but his eyes seemed glazed, his speech was faint and lacked coherence. His dark golden skin was gradually turning flame-red. He looked discomfited, but he didn't feel hot. His heartbeat had increased dramatically since the night before, but for all I knew that might mean absolutely nothing.

Mercede had also begun to sicken. She claimed that she was all right, but I thought that this might be an instance of the language proving misleading. There were all sorts of things the phrase could be taken to mean.

I prowled around outside, feeling slightly angry, trying to sort out the implications of Max's desertion. I knew which way he had gone—there was only one trail of destroyed vegetation, and that was the one which Danel had ploughed. Max had gone after him.

Eve came out to join me.

'What if he doesn't come back either?' she asked.

'Well,' I said acidly, 'what if he doesn't, *captain*? We now have no gun, no call circuit and two sick natives. We are right in the shit without a shovel. What *do* we do, captain?'

I was in a bad mood.

She was impressed by the waspishness in my outburst, but pride wouldn't allow her to retreat.

'You're the specialist in alien environments,' she said. 'You're the ace survivor. I only give the orders. You're supposed to provide the advice.'

'Thanks,' I said. 'The only way your false rank ever comes in useful is to make it easier for you to pass the buck to me. Privilege, hey? How do you feel about the loneliness of command?'

'You're a bastard, Grainger,' she said. Pretty coolly, I thought.

'Yeah,' I said. 'But you love me anyway.'

'An arrogant bastard,' she amended.

'That as well,' I conceded.

She went back inside, leaving me to savour my bitter mood alone. I think the buck was already resting securely in my arms.

Onward, I remarked sardonically, Christian soldiers.

How many? asked the wind.

One, I told him. Who else can I reasonably take?

Eve will expect to go with you.

Fuck Eve.

Some other time, he said.

You have got a sense of humour, I accused.

It wasn't mine, he assured me. It was yours.

But I hadn't time to mess about with fancy remarks. I'd been sitting around too long. I wanted to be up and away. I began to pack.

Eve came to find me just as I'd got everything tied up into a neat bundle.

'Where do you think you're going?' she asked.

'After him,' I said. 'Where else?'

'Like hell you are,' she said.

I was genuinely amazed. 'But you just told me it was all up to me,' I complained. 'I'm the expert, remember? I give the advice, okay? Well, I'm taking it as well. I'm going after him. You and Linda stay here.'

'We wait,' she said.

'I can't.'

'The question I asked you,' she reminded me, 'was: "What if he doesn't come back?" We'll wait first and see if he *does* come back.'

'How long?' I demanded. 'Another day? Another week? Hell,

we've no weapons, no caller, no nothing. Just food and water. If I'm going to sit around in the middle of a jungle, I want adequate equipment. I'm going after Max bloody Volta-Tartaglia if only to get his bloody gun.'

'Stay here,' she said. She didn't have to add anything. I knew perfectly well it was an order. I proceeded to disobey it. I marched out of the tent.

Straight into the arms of Max Volta-Tartaglia.

It just wasn't my day.

He didn't give me time to speak. 'It's a good job you're ready,' he said. 'We've got to get back to Danel in a hurry. I wasn't expecting to find him clapped out. He's dead weight, and we're going to have to carry him. The bugs have definitely got to him. He needs help quickly.'

I was very tempted to lose my temper. But it would only have made matters worse.

'Don't you think,' I said mildly, exercising masterful control, 'that you could have notified us that you were going? Don't you think that it would have been friendly to leave the caller? Also the gun? You're playing silly games with our *lives*.'

'I couldn't leave the caller or the gun,' he said. 'You know I've got orders.'

'*Orders*!' I spat. 'What about discretion? How about *reason*?'

'I knew you'd be all right,' he said confidently. 'I was only going to be gone a couple of hours. It took a bit longer than I thought. I should have been back before morning, along with Danel. I was sure he'd stop when he found out he couldn't make it.'

'*Why didn't you tell us?*' I hissed.

He shrugged. 'Didn't seem necessary,' he said.

I knew damn well that the reason he hadn't told us was that we'd had an argument not long before he'd decided to set out on the joyride. But it didn't make sense, even if it was the reason, and there was no point in airing it right now. We had to get back on the road.

'Okay,' I said. 'Let's move. But this time leave the gun and the caller.'

'Not the gun,' he said. 'They were very insistent about the gun. But I'll leave the caller. Fair enough?'

It wasn't, but what was the point in arguing?

We compromised, and we set off.

It took me five miles to walk the burn out of my seething anger. It took another seven or more before the trail we were following suddenly thinned out.

A glance at Max served to confirm my suspicion. We had got there. And the cupboard was bare.

'This is where he was,' said Max. 'I swear it.'

'What did you leave with him?' I asked.

'Nothing. He was out cold. There was no point.'

'What did you take away from him?'

'Nothing,' he said again. 'I....'

'I know,' I said. 'You didn't see the point. So he still has the gun as well as the axe. But no food and no water.'

'I guess so.'

'Thanks for the confirmation,' I said. 'Well, there's no point in hanging around. He went thataway.'

I pointed in the direction of the trail. It was the same direction he had been heading before. It was a good direction. Straight as a die. Anyone else wandering around in a forest with trees so big that visibility was never more than thirty yards would have wandered about erratically. But without a compass, Danel was taking the shortest route to wherever he wanted to go.

'He must be delirious,' said Max.

'Or determined,' I said. 'What's he heading for, do you know?'

'There's supposed to be a mountain,' said Max. 'Not a big one. The ground rises quite a bit as we go into the forest from here. The trees still maintain total cover, but the undergrowth isn't so thick higher up. But I don't know for sure that's where he's headed. For all I know he's just going on and on without any idea of a destination.'

I decided to hope that wasn't true.

I began to walk on.

'Wait,' he said. 'I think you ought to go back.'

'Why?' I asked.

'They'll be expecting us back at the camp. The situation's changed and they ought to be informed. So should home base. We can't just go on walking forever. We can't rely on finding Danel today.'

'This burst of consideration,' I pointed out, 'seems most out of character.'

'Okay,' he said. 'Okay, so I should have told you where I went last night. If you must know, I only intended to take a short walk. It wasn't until I'd gone a couple of miles that I decided to keep going. That's why I didn't take any of the supplies or leave the caller. Well, now things are different, aren't they? We have to think things out. I'll find him, if possible. If it's not, I'll come back. You'll be all right, if you sit tight. Base will send the copter out to you. If you complain about the arms situation, they might even relent enough to drop you another gun.'

I didn't want to go on alone, because this struck me as being a potential wild goose chase anyhow. Therefore, I decided, if anyone was going back it had better be me. And someone ought to go back—I was sure enough of that. I made a mental note to write the whole of the farce out of my memory at the earliest possible moment. Everything had gone wrong for some time now. The whole expedition looked like a washout. Not even a hard-fought failure. Just a deflatory collapse. I was in the right frame of mind to jack it all in and go home, at that particular moment.

Wearily, I began to trudge back along the well-worn trail. I was far from happy. It seemed like a long way.

About a mile from camp, I noticed a sudden profusion of cropper tracks criss-crossing the trail. They had not been there on the outward journey. We had seen cropper tracks often during the previous few days. They came in all sizes—the term just meant 'harmless animal' or something like it. They didn't make anywhere near the mess of the ground cover that we did, of course, unless they were cow-sized and moving in sizeable herds, but they always left a noticeable track. The undergrowth was very quick to regenerate, but the track was always obvious for a day or two.

There was nothing particularly sinister about finding a lot of cropper tracks intersecting our trail, but they did seem slightly odd. Herds of croppers moved in single file, as a rule, so that they didn't trample more vegetation than was necessary. But this herd—if it had been a herd and not several groups—had been moving with a much greater degree of independence.

Almost as if they had been in too much of a hurry to stick to the etiquette of the situation.

Within half a mile of the camp, I began to hear noises. It was a distant rustling. It seemed to be coming from a fairly wide range of direction. I wasted no time in building up a healthy degree of fright. There was something nasty in the vicinity, and I was unarmed. So was the camp. I took the knife from my belt, not because I anticipated its proving useful, but because it made me feel better.

I didn't run, but I moved forward quickly.

There was a noise of somebody running, and almost as I heard it, I saw who it was.

It was Mercede, and she was coming toward me as fast as she could go. She didn't seem to see me. She seemed to have every intention of passing right by me and running forever. She was running away from something that she was very frightened of indeed. My first thought was spiders, but then I remembered Max's offhand dismissal of the things he called magna-drivers.

Driver ants. Large ones.

I moved into her way, and called her name. She looked at me, suddenly, without any expression in her face. Then she cannoned into me.

I caught her and held her still. She didn't struggle, but seemed glad of the opportunity to collapse, as though she were signing her fate over to me. I don't know whether she knew me, or whether she thought I was Danel, or whether she cared.

I stared into her face, and her blind eyes stared back. For a moment, I thought that she was simply stricken by fear, but then I began to suspect that she really was blind.

But there was no time to explore the problem in depth. The enemy was coming. I didn't know whether to go toward the camp, back the way I had come, or away from the general direction of the sound, which was almost at right angles to our course.

'Where are the others?' I barked. 'Tell me.'

'Mmmm...,' she gasped.

'Magna-drivers,' I filled in for her. 'I know that. What about Linda and Eve and Micheal?'

She shook her head violently. I moved slightly, in the direction of the camp. She grabbed hold of me, and she wouldn't let me go. I realised that the sound now filled nearly a full quadrant of direction. From just left of the trail to the camp to just right of an intersect across that trail. And it was getting louder.

'We can't stay here!' I shouted at her.

She clung hard to my arm.

'I've got to go back,' I told her. I lacked conviction. I didn't want to go toward the sound of rustling.

'No,' she said. 'They ran. All ran. All ran.'

And they hadn't run together. The idiots. But there were the trees, of course. It's far too easy to get separated in a forest if you're in a hurry. Especially if you're in a panic.

'We've got to get out of the way,' I said. Not to Mercede—she already knew that. I was talking out loud, to excuse the fact that I was about to turn coward and run away.

'Go,' she said. 'Go fast.'

And so we went. It was no time for hesitating, no matter how much doubt I was in. I glanced back over my shoulder, and I couldn't see a thing. But I could still hear that rustling getting louder, and I could readily imagine it was the clicking of a thousand pairs of well-oiled scissors—a murmurous clickety-click. Jaws clicking.

We turned and we ran, hand in hand. I steered us along our own personal highway. I don't know how she managed to stick to the highway while she was running away from the camp, because it became quickly obvious that she was quite sightless.

She kept dragging me away to the right, away from the noise. Two or three minutes served to convince me that she was probably right. There was no point in following the trail. Avoiding our pursuers had to take priority over all else. We began to put substantial distance in between ourselves and the nasties. They weren't very fast. The sound did begin to die away.

It didn't matter too much that we were getting lost. We were all lost. The trip wasn't just a washout any more. It was an incipient tragedy. The *Zodiacs* had overplayed their hand. They had insisted that it was all easy, all under control. They had insisted that there was no danger, that nothing would go wrong.

If I ever survived to say 'I told you so'—to Denton, to Max, or to anybody else—I would be lucky. Nothing short of luck could save us now. I felt sick, because luck is one thing I always hope that I never have to rely on.

I don't believe in it.

We kept falling over. The root-ridges seemed to be deployed with the specific intention of tripping us up at every opportunity.

Every time we fell over, we got scared about the amount of time it was costing us, the amount of wind it was knocking out of us, and the pounding it was giving our bones and our muscles.

I don't know how long we staggered and stumbled around after we were just too plain shattered to run any more. We kept going, certainly, for a matter of hours. There was nothing at all to be gained by stopping to think. I knew I might as well run off the adrenaline, and Mercede showed no inclination at all to stop. She seemed almost hypnotised, consumed by the same relentless determination which had taken Danel far away from us into the jungle.

We lost the sound of the magna-drivers, but that didn't affect the situation at all. We weren't running because of magna-drivers. We were running because of fear and emotional momentum. You always run when you're scared, and you keep running while there's something you don't want to look in the face, and it doesn't really matter whether the thing you don't want to stare down is a magna-driver or the idea of your own running away. Running breeds running, and you run till you drop for the last time.

My heart hurt, my thigh muscles were knotted with cramp, but somehow I managed to keep going just so long as Mercede remained tireless. She wasn't any more scared than I was, and certainly no fitter. It was her sickness that was doing her the favour of carrying her on and on without reference to her will. I knew that when she dropped she would drop for good—or for a good long while—like Danel had. I had to wait for that to happen, or it would lose her.

The wind kept on going. My chest felt spring-loaded, my legs were red-hot. He was no painkiller. But I moved, and matched her movement. We finished up running uphill, and the undergrowth was getting thicker and deeper.

It all ended when we fell down a crevice, and landed feet first up to our necks in the stuff. It held us up simply because it was too densely packed to let us fall.

I let go of her hand.

About an hour later, as it was getting dark, I contrived to extricate myself, and then to prise her loose. Instead of clearing—or attempting to clear—a patch of ground, I climbed up onto a big root, and pulled us slowly up to the junction of root and trunk. We were a comfortable two feet above the undergrowth, and the root was wide enough for us to lie full length without the danger of rolling off if we twitched. I laid Mercede out, but I elected to curl myself up in a foetal sitting position, with my back supported by the gigantic bole of the tree.

Darkness fell. I had a flashlight in my pack, but I didn't bother to fish it out. I was content to wait.

For the morning or the monsters. Whichever arrived first.

CHAPTER THIRTEEN

THE MORNING WON. WE heard nothing remotely suggestive of the whispering which threatened the approach of the magna-drivers. In all my time on Chao Phrya I never saw one of those supposedly loathsome creatures, but the fact of their existence nevertheless contrived to play a considerable part in the drama that was acted out upon that world. I have rarely been so scared, because I have rarely been so presumably helpless. What you can see is never quite so bad as what lurks outside your line of sight while maintaining the constant threat of a terrifying invasion. Nothing real is fearful. We are only scared of our images.

When morning came, Mercede seemed to me to be very ill indeed. There was no great physical change manifest, save for the deepening of her skin colour from soft gold to angry red. She was neither hot not desiccated, so far as I could tell. Her breathing was laboured, though, and she was unconscious. She moved a little in her heavy sleep, but I never had to struggle to keep her on our perch above the threadbare sea of fungus. She moaned, but never coherently. It did not seem to me that she was moaning in the thin, shapeless language of her people.

There was nothing I could do but sit and wait until she was well enough to wake of her own accord. I could not carry her—she was as tall as me and about as heavy—and I didn't want to force her to wake and walk.

We had some food, and a little water—they remained from the packsack I had taken with me on the abortive attempt to recover Danel—but they would hardly last us more than a day or two. Perhaps Mercede could live off the land, if she knew how to, but it would be very difficult for me. The fact that humans could metabolise a certain fraction of Chao Phrya's produce only made it more dangerous to select potential foods at random. Where there are metabolites, there are inevitably poisons.

You survived for two years on Lapthorn's Grave, the wind reminded me.

I had some gruel to help me, I said. I had some medical supplies. And I spent a great deal of time being sick. It was a long, hard process, clearing even that sparse vegetation which grew on the black mountain. I don't think I can afford to be incapacitated here.

I stared morosely up into the purple prismatic roof of the forest, letting my eyes drift along the branch lines and measure the spacing of the giant trunks. We were definitely on a considerable slope, but the forest took the declivity in its stride. I could see no gap in the translucent canopy, and no hint of an end to it as I looked up the slope. The hill was completely immersed, so far as I could tell.

The undergrowth layer was very uneven on the slope, as Max had suggested with reference to the mountain where the wild Anacaona might be found. I did not think that this might be that same mountain. We had not come far enough, and we had come in the wrong direction. I occupied some time in plotting a course which would eventually take us away from our vantage point up the hill without involving us with any clump of fungus of appreciable size. But it was a hollow pursuit. The twisting path would take in far too much wasted distance. Far better to plunge straight on through the fungus and the matted feeble stalks. They were too weak to obstruct our passage with more than a gesture of resistance.

I found the waiting very wearing. The seriousness of the situation seemed to forbid any conversation with the wind. It was obvious that escape from the forest was now our only priority, and it was equally obvious that we were unlikely to be able to achieve it without substantial help—presumably from the wild Anacaona. The question of what to do resolved itself into the question of where to look. I had no idea. Mercede might know, but it was more likely that she wouldn't. Our best hope seemed to be that one or more of the others might find, or be found by, the forest people, and that a search would be mounted for the rest of us. At least I had no reason to doubt the good will of the forest people. If the woman and the girl were with the forest people, they might be called upon to find us, rather than our finding them. This seemed an ironic eventuality, but I hardly knew what to expect of the Anacaona even after all the time I had spent trying to understand them, and somehow it did not strike me as being a particularly unbelievable outcome.

As time wore on, however, my morbid general outlook on the situation as a whole was replaced by a more immediate concern for Mercede's wellbeing.

What are the odds, I wondered silently, that she stays comatose all day and we have to spend another night perched up here?

It's wait for her or leave her, commented the wind dourly. And you don't have anywhere to go.

I contemplated trying to make some kind of a signal.

Only fools start fires in forests, was the wind's only contribution to this chain of thought.

I knew—and so did he—that doing absolutely nothing was as far from my style as one could possibly get. That's why there had been such a deterioration in my personality during the two years I was stuck on Lapthorn's Grave. My mind had been asleep during those two years, and I had been very slow waking up even after Axel Cyran and his merry men picked me up after mistaking me for the *Lost Star*. I wasn't quite right yet, in some ways. I still had vague feelings of emptiness, although nothing like the vacuous days on the rock or the tortuous misanthropic time I went through on Earth almost immediately afterward.

It won't be too long, the wind promised. If she doesn't come out of it soon to eat and drink, she'll die. Then you'll have to move on your own.

Which was true enough, though very unpleasant. There was nothing I could do for her except try to pour a little water into her now and again, which I did.

Eventually, to save the pain of waiting, I went back to sleep.

CHAPTER FOURTEEN

I AWOKE IN THE early evening. For a second or two, I did not know what had wakened me. Then I realised that it had been a sound. The sound was still there—it was very faint but it was quite unmistakable.

It was the sound of Micheal's pipes. It was a strong contender for the title of the sound which I most wanted to hear at that particular time. It signified new hope. If Micheal was near enough to be heard, then he was near enough to be found. If he was well enough to play, then he was well enough to think. His thinking stood a far better chance of getting us out of this mess than did mine.

I stood up and yelled at the top of my voice. The abruptness of my movement made me feel suddenly giddy, and the giddiness cut off my cry in mid-syllable, strangling it to a whimper. But I called his name a second time, and listened to the echoes bounding off the tree trunks. I knew how deceptive distance and direction can be when you're trying to follow a sound in a forest, so I kept shouting at five-second intervals, listening for the music of the panpipes in between.

For an unbearably long time (at least two minutes) the sound of the music grew no louder at all. Then it stopped altogether. I took this as a sign that the import of my shouting had broken Micheal's concentration at last, and that he would be free to respond. I continued shouting, trying as best I could to maintain the volume of my cries.

Darkness was falling around us, and I grew scared that he

might not be able to find us in the dark. That was a totally irrational fear, of course, but it made me kneel to fish in my packsack for the flashlight. I began to wave the light around in a wide arc, so that its light could flicker in between the tree trunks. It was not a very useful gesture—the trees would cut the light out completely less than forty yards away.

But the shouting served its purpose. At last, Micheal appeared. He was moving slowly, almost drunkenly. His fingers snaked up and down the pipes even though they were no longer applied to his lips. It was as though he was following the series of variations which he had been playing, even though the sounds were purely theoretical.. His eyes seemed wide and staring, but that was probably an illusion of the light. He came closer and closer, moving like an automaton toward me. He couldn't see me. Like Mercede, he was blind.

I stopped calling, and listened to the echoes dying away.

He faltered in his stride, and hesitated, waiting for another call to guide his steps.

'Micheal,' I said, in the best approximation I could manage to a normal voice. 'We're here. Up on a root. Can't you see the light?'

He heard me, and I saw his face change slightly as he realised that he had found me. His fingers slowed their sinuous silent dance, and I saw the effort of will which it took to order them to stop.

He had no packsack with him. No food. No water.

He looked up at me, and suddenly his eyes could see again. I *saw* him begin to see me. He nodded his head.

'You can see me now,' I said.

'Not very well,' he answered. 'But I can see.'

'Mercede's blind,' I said. 'She's been unconscious for a full day. We ran away from the magna-drivers.'

'I know,' he said.

'Have you seen the others?' I asked. 'Eve? Linda?'

'I was with Eve,' he told me. 'I lost her.'

'Was she hurt?'

'No. Have you any food?'

'A little,' I said. 'But I don't know how much of it is good for you. Can you eat our food?'

'I think so,' he said. 'We can get water from the river.'

'River?'

'It isn't far. I was near it when you shouted. Can you let me have some food? Then we can take Mercede to the river.'

He pointed away to his right, diagonally up the slope.

I threw the packsack down to him, and jumped down to join him. He found a bare patch of ground and sat down to rummage in the pack.

'I don't know whether Mercede can be moved,' I said. 'Do you think it'll be all right to make her wake up?'

He put the pipes to his lips, and frowned briefly. Then he played a short tune—not in any way like the long, leisurely music which I had heard him play before. These notes were harsh and penetrating. The insistent quality in the music was answered immediately as Mercede revived from her semi-comatose state, shook her head and then slowly rolled herself around on the root-ridge, stretching her muscles. Then she oozed into a kneeling position and began to stand. I offered her a hand and helped her get down from the root.

She joined Micheal, but I knew as I steadied her with my hand and passed her on to him that she was still blind. I directed the flashlight beam at her face, but there was no response.

'Can you give her back her sight?' I asked, feeling at that particular moment as if nothing ought to be beyond the power of the pipes.

But he shook his head.

We divided the food which remained equally between the three of us. Micheal inspected it all carefully, and decided that there was nothing which could not be equally appreciated by either of our races. There was not very much.

'All right,' I said, when we had finished, 'What do we do now?'

'The river,' he said.

'And then?'

'We'll find the forest people.' Just like that. Micheal was supremely confident. And yet Mercede was still blind, and both of them were still sick.

'Do you know anything at all about the others?' I asked him. 'Could the magna-drivers have caught up with them?'

'I don't think so,' he said. 'We knew what was happening. We all ran. As long as they ran fast enough, they're safe. From the magna-drivers, at least.'

'What will happen to them?'

He shrugged. 'If they find the forest people, or the forest people find them, they'd be all right'

'If not?'

He shrugged his shoulders again. I knew as well as he did. It was a big forest. Danel could have reached the forest people by now. Or Max. But would they know where we were likely to be? And could they know that there was any urgency about finding us?

As we set off for the river, he put the pipes to his lips again, and began to blow soft, whispering notes in a slow, languid melody. As he played, his eyes changed again. I waved my hand in front of them—first apologetically, then in earnest. He was blind again. He had resigned the effort of maintaining the connection between mind and eye. I realised that he must be able to use the music of the pipes as a sonar system. There had to be a direct mode of communication between the music and the mind—the mode by which he had made Mercede wake from her deep sleep, and the mode by which he hypnotised spiders for Danel.

Like the Pied Piper of Hamelin he led us through the jungle, forcing his way through the deeper undergrowth with hips and elbows while his fingers never paused in their ceaseless ebb and flow. The music he played spun out into a modulated chain of delicate sounds which put me in mind of wind and water. I didn't like it. In a concert hall or coming out of the HV it might have given me a nostalgic image of the great outdoors. But here we were actually at the mercy of the great outdoors and I was far from nostalgic. The mood of the music fit the moment too well. It was a bad moment. We were still in trouble.

The water was very welcome, but it tasted sour. Micheal came back to the land of the living for a while in order to participate.

'Do we rest until morning now?' I asked him.

'No.'

It was the answer I wanted to hear. I didn't like the idea of wasting any more time at all, but I would have been prepared to rest had he thought that Mercede couldn't walk throughout the night.

The fact that it was dark, of course, wouldn't bother either of them.

'Which way do we go?' I asked.

'Upriver,' he told me. He didn't add any kind of an explanation. The hill must be bigger than I thought—perhaps the slope went up into the mountains after all. The idea of walking uphill all night wasn't too appealing, but our way would be fairly easy because there was a narrow strip on either side of the 'river'—it was really only a stream—where the undergrowth grew horizontally rather than vertically. It was like a thick-piled carpet, and by no means a barrier to progress.

I helped Mercede to rise as Micheal began fingering the pipes pensively.

'Are you all right?' I asked her. I was whispering, anticipating that Micheal would begin to play any second, and not wanting my voice to clash with the fragile spell of the pipes.

'All right,' she assured me.

'We can keep going,' said Micheal.

I didn't really want to start an intellectual conversation at such an inopportune moment, but I couldn't resist saying, 'How the hell d'you do it?'

'We have to keep moving,' he said.

'Those pipes might put you in the right frame of mind,' I said. 'But they can't give you the strength and the stamina. If you use them to drive you on and on, they'll kill you in the end, surely?'

'The sickness will feed me,' he said.

'How?'

'It accelerates the breakdown of stored energy,' he said.

We had already got far enough for the point. I let the matter drop. If he said he could keep going, and Mercede too, I was willing to believe them.

'I'd better go first,' I said. 'I don't want either of you falling in the water. I can't swim.'

I thought it might be a good idea if Mercede placed her hand on my shoulder, and Micheal located himself in the rear, using his pipes. But Mercede apparently wasn't keen on the idea of touching me. We'd held each other the previous night, but that had been while we were in the grip of panic. In cold blood, she couldn't bring herself to do it.

So I set off, and left them to make their own arrangements for sticking together.

Well, I said to the wind, what price Captain Lapthorn, ace crimebuster, now? The *Zodiac* mob appears to have facilitated an almighty mess. Won't Charlot be delighted?

If you find the forest people, he said, you appear to have pretty much the same chance of finding Alyne and her kidnapper as you ever did.

Maybe so, I said. But we're still no closer to being able to guess what sort of a chance that was. We know next to nothing about the crime, the possible motive, and the possible reactions of any other parties who might come to be involved. What chance would Sherlock Holmes have, working under our conditions? Pretty slim, I'll bet.

Depends on his powers of deduction.

Okay, Sherlock, I said. Deduce. Don't just make patronising remarks. Explain all to me.

I can't.

Thanks a lot.

Suppose the girl *were* an Indris, he said.

I've tried supposing it, I assured him.

And?

So what?

So she's a descendant of an ancient starfaring species which no longer maintains any kind of interstellar contact. They might be all dead, but it's simpler to think that they just went home, or went somewhere else entirely. That's irrelevant for the moment. The Anacaona are a degenerate line, adapted either by evolution or by engineering to this world. The girl is a throwback a long, long way. What does that suggest to you?

Genetic interference, I said.

He didn't say anything else. His case was resting.

The woman isn't her mother, Charlot had told me. That made it kidnap. But who was the child's mother? Anybody? The idea filled me with a wondrous inspiration for all of a minute before I realised that it didn't really mean a thing. It didn't advance our thinking one iota. It didn't offer us a motive. It didn't shed any new light on the attitude of the forest people.

What it did do was cast a little new light on Titus Charlot. Even in my most cynical moods, I had never really believed that Charlot was taking gross liberties with his guests at the Anacaon colony. I had believed his assurances that he was working co-operatively toward a greater understanding between the species, and toward a synergistic commingling of knowledge and thought. But if what the wind thought was true, it cast new—and to my mind distasteful—light on the whole method of approach which Charlot adopted to these ends.

I made a mental note to the effect that a cop named Denton owed me a drink.

Possibly a double.

Dawn came, eventually, and we had found no Anacaona. No nothing, in fact. We just went up and up, alongside the river. The slope was very gentle and very even, and we'd hardly noticed it. But up is up, and over long distances it would undoubtedly take a lot out of us. The music kept Micheal going, and presumably Mercede too. The wind kept me going. I was glad, in a way, that Eve and Linda hadn't managed to join us. I hoped they were together, with enough food and water to keep them going, and enough sense to stick close enough to the old campsite to be found when and if a search was mounted. If they were really lucky, of course, Linda would still have the caller, in which case they wouldn't even be in the same trouble I was.

We rested briefly in the first daylight. Micheal didn't want to, but he concurred in order to oblige me.

He stopped playing.

'Well,' I said. 'How much farther?'

'Not much,' he said.

'We are going somewhere, then?' I said. 'An actual place. We aren't just following the river out of pure optimism?'

'There's a place,' he said.

'Go on,' I said. 'What place?'

'It used to be a city,' he said. 'It's buried now, under the forest. It doesn't look like a city any more. But the forest people often use it. I think they might be there.'

'A *city*? A city in the forest? An Anacaon city?'

'No,' he said calmly—almost absently. 'An Indris city, of course.'

'Linda said there weren't any. No traces. No relics of any kind.'

'She doesn't know,' he said.

'You lied to her then. You hid it from her.'

He shook his head. 'Nobody told her any lies,' he said. 'She didn't want to know.'

So Linda didn't want to know about the Indris. So much for the noble pursuit of pure knowledge. The idea of the Promised Land had already answered all the questions. Don't confuse me with the facts, I've already made up my mind. I shook my head sadly.

The city seemed like an exciting prospect. I'm not one of these people who flip over ruins, but I was ready enough to take a look at anything which offered an alternative to the incredible sameness of the forest. And the thought that it was a definite somewhere that we might possibly expect to find the elusive forest people was an undeniably welcome one.

My natural pessimism, however, put in its usual sterling work in preparing me for disappointment. It doesn't do to pin all your hope to one target. Whatever happens, you always have to keep going. The first principle of survival is the survival of effort.

We found the city, all right. Another couple of hours saw us right into the city square.

It didn't look like a city. The trees grew, the canopy of purple was unbroken, the ground was still covered by the same sort of mess we'd been wading in for a week. But here and there you could scrape away the gunge and find that the surface underneath was stone. Smooth stone. Sculptured stone. The tree trunks and their big roots didn't give a damn about stone—they'd pulverised it with no trouble. Ninety percent of the city was rubble and dust. No buildings remained. But here and there was the memory of a city street.

The city had been dead, I guessed, on the order of tens of thousands of years. But who am I to guess about such things? It might have been a hundred times that. But those trees were *big* and *old*. They hadn't worked their way to perfect mastery of that city in a matter of centuries. They'd invested some real time in it.

The forest people had been there, all right. But they were riot there now.

We'd missed the boat.

CHAPTER FIFTEEN

THE SOLE OCCUPANT OF the buried city was a dead cropper. It was about the size of a cow. I suppose that it fulfilled the same kind of function as a cow. It lay in an open space which had been methodically cleared of all undergrowth—the site of the Anacaon encampment. The trail that the forest people had left when they had decided to move on was like a major highway. It wasn't wide—these people respected the country code and walked in a tight column, using each other's footprints—but it had sure been walked on by a lot of feet. It would take the forest a week or two to reclaim it.

'Is the cropper still fresh?' I asked Micheal. It had seemed that way to me, but I thought I'd better check.

'Yes,' he said, 'but we'd better cook the meat well.'

'It didn't die of anything horrible, did it?' I asked. 'Does it signify anything that the forest people left it untouched?'

He shook his head slightly.

'I don't know,' he said slowly. 'I think it might mean....'

He hesitated, and I completed the thought for him. 'You think they left it for us?'

'Perhaps,' he said. 'But we can't assume that'

'They haven't left a message,' I said. I'm not sure what kind of message I expected. They could hardly have left a sign saying 'Back soon—help yourself.' The Anacaona had no written language. If they had a direct sound-to-mind link, it was quite probable that their language couldn't possibly be written down.

'Is it safe to light a fire?' I asked Micheal.

'Yes,' he said. 'Can you?'

I fished out a light. 'Never travel without one,' I said.

'It can't spread here,' he said, meaning the cleared area.

'Your people had no fire. There are no ashes.'

'They wouldn't light a fire,' he said. 'They don't have the taste for cooked meat that you people have.'

'What about you?'

'We eat meat. Your people have taught mine a great deal.'

The fire wasn't easy to start. The trees didn't drop twigs and the fungus wasn't at all keen to burn. At first we got nothing but a lot of smoke and a foul smell, but persistence eventually paid off and I forced some of the stuff to catch. We gradually built up a convincing blaze in a hollow on a pile of crumbled stone.

I've never been an expert at carving meat, but when you live out on the rim it's one of those things you have to get used to. I set about hacking bits of dead cropper off the carcass, and used my knife to roast it in the flame. It was a slow process, and my hand was painfully close to the flames, but circumstances demanded that the meat be well done, and I kept at it. The alien bacteria were unlikely to attack me, of course—although it was far from impossible, bearing in mind the metabolic overlap between the life systems of Earth and Chao Phrya—but the last thing I wanted was for Micheal and/or Mercede to pick up some secondary infection. Natural resilience and magic music notwithstanding, I knew it would kill them.

Mercede was stretched out on the stone, and Micheal sat beside her, playing softly. I think he was trying to bring her down slowly—play her out of the automatic phase in which the music had sustained her for so long.

We ate in silence. The meat was tough and tasted awful. Owing to my culinary inexpertise it was heavily flavoured with charcoal, but it was such a relief to get something down my throat again that I gladly overlooked its shortcomings.

'How are you feeling?' I asked Micheal, when he rose after offering my canteen to his sister.

'Bad,' he said. I was mildly surprised—he'd been so offhand

before.

'Mercede?' I asked.

'She's recovering slowly. I think we should leave her to sleep. I don't think there's much profit in moving on for a while. We'll be all right here for a while.'

'Do you think they might come back?'

'They might.' His voice was neutral. There was a real possibility, then.

'We'll rest, then,' I said. 'We'll wait here until you think it's safe to continue.'

'Thank you,' he said.

'It's your show,' I told him. 'You're the one who knows what's what. Are you going to try and get some sleep?'

'I don't know that I should,' he said. 'I've relied much more on the music these last days. I'm almost afraid that if I let my body go its own way, my heart might stop.'

I didn't know whether I ought to sympathise with him or not. It would inevitably sound patronising. I didn't know whether he knew me well enough to accept my concern. I didn't have any idea at all what he might think of me. So I lowered my eyes and stayed silent.

'I think I'll have to let the sickness take a hold,' he said. 'If I contain it any longer it will shake me apart when I release it.'

'What does that entail?' I asked him quietly.

'I have to sit very still. I must fight the sickness on my own.'

'No music?'

'No music.'

I didn't doubt that he knew what he was talking about, but I didn't want to question him about it. Far better to let him get on with it. Sometimes you have to be content not to understand. What happens is sometimes far more important than what you think is happening.

Micheal began to settle himself, and then froze suddenly, half-kneeling, half-crouching. His eyes had fixed upon something that was behind me. I could see his face very clearly, all the lines in it emphasised by the way everything stopped, and by the fear which I felt *because* everything stopped. A chill slid slowly down my spine. I began to turn, feeling that I was doing so very slowly, already knowing what it was that was behind me.

'Don't move,' said Micheal. His voice hissed from still lips—although the words were English the tone was the language of the Anacaona. I stopped turning my head. I still couldn't see it.

'Stay just where you are,' added Micheal. 'Relax, so that you can hold yourself still.'

In grotesque slow motion, he took the panpipes from his lap, and raised them to his lips.

He began to play a languorous, intensive melody which sounded like dance music slowed by a factor of three or four. The notes moaned, and lingered in the air. The tune rose and fell like the swell of a turgid sea.

I didn't dare turn my head, because he had told me to be still. But only a few minutes passed before the need to turn was quite gone. There was another emerging from the trees behind Micheal. Then another, away to the left. And another alongside that one.

Eventually, I could see four, and there were probably several more that I couldn't see without looking over my shoulder. Whether it was the blood scent of the dead cropper or the smoke from the fire that had brought them out I didn't know and I couldn't ask. It didn't matter. They were here.

At last.

We had no weapon except for my knife. Micheal's pipes were holding them under a weird kind of spell and I didn't know how strong it was or what kind of action might serve to break it. I didn't know how long he could keep playing in his present state. But I could imagine what might happen if he stopped.

The crypto-arachnids were about the size of black bears, except that their legs were longer and made them look more spread out. They were furred like black bears too. But they had moved like the spiders I knew but had never come to love, with sinuous serial scuttling movements of a multiplicity of legs.

Their mouths were hairy, and equipped with a large number of appendages for cutting and pulping food before sucking it in via twin sphincters. I couldn't see any eyes. They had no eyestalks like Earthly spiders, but they might have had any number of ocelli set within their fur. There was no way of knowing. Perhaps they had real eyes, but small and deep-set like a mole's. They couldn't rely too much on sight in the purple jungle, but they were obviously sensitive to movement or Micheal would not have insisted that I be still.

The sheer helplessness of my position was appalling. Micheal simply hadn't had any time to tell me what I should or shouldn't do. I didn't even know whether there was anything I could do. I tried to remember what I'd been told about Danel's semi-ritual methods of spiderhunting. Micheal hypnotised the spiders, Danel slew them—that was all I knew. Danel had to move to axe the spiders, but how fast—or how slowly—did he have to move? What exactly were the risks and how did he counter them?

Could I simply get up and walk around the cleared area—which had now become a kind of arena—and hack the spiders to death with my knife?

What do I *do*? I cried, silently.

Take it easy, said the wind. Take it very slowly. Move in time to the music.

That, at least, sounded sensible. Move in time with the music. It was a rational basis for experiment. But the music was far too slow, its rhythm too tortuous. I couldn't possibly blend my movements with it.

Slow, then. Whatever you do, just make sure it's very, very slow. I'll help you.

I daren't think slowly. My mind was racing. What the hell could I do? Don't try and hack them to death, I admonished myself. One blow is all you dare try. Danel kills in a single blow. The spell of the music won't make them stand still for more than one bang. Hit them with something big. A big rock.

My eyes darted around to the place where we'd built the fire.

Out of the corner of my eye I surveyed the heap of rubble. There were several big rocks there. I had to select one that I could lift and carry, but also one which would make no mistake in crushing the life out of a two-ton spider. It seemed like a hopeless task, but I knew that a two-ton exoskeletal would be a great deal more fragile than a big mammal or reptile. A more urgent problem might easily be: Could I extract a suitable rock without making the whole pile slip and causing an unwanted flurry of movement?

Was there anything else I could do?

You can ask, said the wind.

Micheal can't answer.

Mercede?

She'll be unconscious for hours, and she might not be able to help anyway.

If in doubt, the wind reminded me, hesitate.

I'm hesitating, I assured him. I'm hesitating. But the heat's on. I don't know that I have any time in hand at all.

I knew that I might wreck everything with a false move, but there was no way I could guard against the false moves in advance. I could only make absolutely sure in my own mind that I knew exactly what I was going to do before I did it, and what I was going to do if I found out halfway through that it wasn't going to work.

I had to do something, or we were all as good as dead anyway.

I looked at Micheal, but he was entranced by his own music. He couldn't see me. He couldn't even look frightened. There was an awful intensity in his expression as he blew steadfastly across the mouth of the pipes.

That boy is seriously ill, I reminded myself. He said not ten minutes ago that he had to let the sickness take a hold—that if he tried to hold it in much longer it would shake him apart when he released it. Can he still be holding it? Is this the right music? Can it do both jobs at once, or is he about to give under the strain?

How long, I wondered, could he keep it up? Hours? Minutes?

All night?

All right, said the wind, adding his weight to the argument I'd already built up. *Move.*

I let my head complete the turn which it had begun some minutes earlier. The crypto-arachnid behind me was just fifteen feet away from me. It was perched on top of a shoulder of loose rock, disturbed by a root-ridge. It was poised, held in a bizarre stepping position with one long leg extended to lead it down the slope to where I sat.

There were three more that I hadn't been able to see.

That made eight in all.

I redirected my attention to the one which was nearest. The perfect slab of rock lay just beneath its feet, broken away from the stone apron by the invading root. But to get it I would have to get close enough to the spider's jaws to kiss it.

Very tentatively, I raised myself to my feet.

The wind didn't whisper in my ear—as always he let me get on with the job—but I was conscious of his presence, not only in my mind but in my movements. I mustered all of my concentration to keep tight control over my movements, but I was subject to a persistent niggling temptation to drop the exaggerated slowness in favour of a panic-driven run.

I didn't stand fully erect, but maintained a half-crouch, and moved crabwise toward the spider. It seemed easier to move one arm and leg out toward it, and then close up my rear arm and leg. The bulk of my movement was thus in a plane directed straight at the spider, and might not be so noticeable from the creature's point of view.

Though I was terribly careful about the snail-like quality of my motion, it seemed that hardly any time at all had passed when I found myself level with the spider's extended foreleg. I looked down at it. It was as thick as my leg. It had a huge hairy clubfoot. Beneath the coarse hair the chitinous exoskeleton had a purple sheen.

The foot moved.

I didn't.

I undoubtedly owe my life to the fact that the utter shock of that moment did not spur me to instant recoil. I remained frozen, and the spider relapsed into stillness.

I was even more careful as I crouched right down and inched forward into the shadow of the monster. I could smell its breath—sweet and heavy, not really unpleasant. I could see the myriad tiny movements of its complicated mouthparts—quite automatic and beyond its control, but nevertheless frightening and apparently threatening. I could almost sense the tension in its limbs as the muscles held it in an unnatural posture.

My hands gripped the slab. I began to pull it backward, praying that I had not misjudged its weight either way. As it slid along; the ground it made a thin grating noise, and the spider drew back its extended leg. Once again, my control held, and as soon as I paused it stopped. But there was no alternative but to keep dragging the rock clear. It was light enough for me to pick up, but it would be a considerable weightlifting feat by my standards, and I would need the space to pluck it from the ground and smack the spider with it all in one smooth motion. There was no question of lifting it free from the ground while I pulled it out from beneath the monster.

As the steady scrape began again, the spider relaxed. But its movements were as tortuous as my own. The interference between the scraping of the slab and the music was so very slight that it barely gave the spider any freedom of will at all. All these movements were almost entirely the work of reflex.

Finally, the slab was clear of the spider's bulk, resting where the extended foot had been resting only a few moments before. I gripped it securely in my arms, and measured the position of the spider's head and thorax with my eyes, until I was sure I knew exactly what trajectory the boulder was to be called upon to take.

Then I began to lift. For one horrible instant I was afraid that my fatigued muscles were going to prove inadequate to the task. But my wind-assisted strength merely needed gathering. I lifted the slab, past my waist, past my chest, and finally above my head. Its sheer mass made me sway a little, and there was an inevitable pause between chest and head as I prepared my arms for the extension and shifted my grip. Both these factors modified the smoothness of the action, and by the time I released the missile into its downward course, the spider had moved, with a slithering shuffle of its eight legs, fully three feet toward me. The rock bounced, not onto the junction of head and thorax as I had intended, but onto the abdomen. It landed edge first, the exoskeleton cracked audibly, and the rock pivoted about the point of impact and fell forward. The other edge smashed the head into the ground only an inch from my toes. I had to move backward. The spider died instantly, but its reflexes did not. Its legs vibrated convulsively for ten seconds or more. One of them shook itself clean off the body.

Except for the panpipes, absolute silence followed the thud of the falling boulder, but the death throes of the crypto-arachnid and my backward step and the fall of the rock all added up to a considerable, if localised, flurry of movement.

When I turned around—slowly—to look at the other spiders, they were all several feet closer. They had been caught again in the restored stillness, but they had all made ground.

The nearest one was now only seven or eight yards from Micheal, and the most distant was not more than thirty. It would have taken a mathematical genius to work out how much each of them would gain every time I tried to kill one. At a rough guess, I thought I might just make it if I conceded them no more than the minimum each time. But I didn't have a monopoly on movement. Every time one of the creatures died, it would make its contribution to our collective downfall.

As I stooped to pick up the slab from the wreckage of the arachnid's foreparts, it responded to my touch with another burst of purely automatic movement. I saw another spider go through a half-shuffle which brought it eighteen inches forward in its course.

I knew, also, that the rock would get heavier the farther I carried it, that my movements must inevitably lose their smoothness.

And the tune faltered.

This shock was so totally unexpected and so hideously ominous that I failed to drown my reaction. I dropped the slab. If it had fallen on my toes, it would have been the death of me. But my legs were widely spaced, and it fell between them.

The spiders gained another stride apiece.

It was hopeless.

I froze immediately, but freezing didn't do much good. Micheal was losing the thread of his music. He was giving way. The disease was getting to him. His concentration was breaking.

He rallied, but I knew that any chance I might have had to kill the spiders was now stone dead.

I had one possible escape. I could walk away, *very* slowly, through the ring of predators, to the edge of the forest. I could duck between the trees and I could run like hell. Even if they chased me, I had a good chance of dodging them. I could cross the river. They couldn't.

I'm no hero. I never claimed to be a hero. If I'd started immediately, I could have made it. But I didn't start. Not because I'm a hero, but rather the reverse. I was scared. I hesitated. And lost my chance.

Micheal faltered again, and the spiders came on. They came very slowly, but they kept coming. They weren't in any hurry, and perhaps it was still worth a try at the dead run. But I couldn't help myself. I backed up in front of them, and before I had time to think I was right next to Micheal.

I looked down at him, and I looked over his shoulder at Mercede. He was just about to fall over. She was sleeping like a baby, oblivious to it all.

I took the panpipes from his lips. Gently. He didn't resist.

As the enemy prepared for the kill, I put them to my own lips.

I think it's your show, I said to the wind. I'm tone deaf.

CHAPTER SIXTEEN

THE WIND WAS GOOD. We weren't up to Micheal's standard, but we didn't have his trick fingers. We were good enough for the spiders, though—I guess they had simple minds. We didn't attempt to play exactly the same piece of music—we settled for something a little simpler and a lot more repetitive. We hadn't the time or the ability to sort out all the variations on our theme and string them together. Once we knew we had something that worked, we set about milking it to death. We tried to duplicate Micheal's style, and in that we seemed to be moderately effective.

I felt somewhat detached from the whole process. It was the first time I'd actually sat back within my body and let the wind do his stuff. I was unconscious in the Drift when he landed the *Hooded Swan*, and all the rest of his work had been covert or subversive.

It was an odd feeling to be a conscious passenger, but it didn't feel anywhere near as bad as I'd expected it might. It was almost as though I was frozen still, like the spiders—not against my will, but because I felt that I daren't move or even think too loudly in case the inner conflict wrecked the wind's co-ordination. I was bent on becoming a mental foetus—as small and as insignificant as possible.

The important thing was that I was willing, and that I was easy in my mind about the whole thing. I didn't exactly love the wind, but you don't have to be in love to know you're on the same side. I still had my lingering fears about being 'taken over,' but familiarity had taken the edge off the fear. The wind and I had lived too long together to be at war.

I stared coolly through the eyes whose movements I no longer controlled. I could see four spiders. One was dead. That left three lurking behind us. I couldn't remember which one was which and which one was the closest. I thought it was one of the ones I couldn't see.

I felt Micheal sag to the ground beside me. He lay very still, his body curled around my feet.

Once the novelty of the situation wore off, I became uncomfortably aware of the fact that what we were doing had a distinct flavour of staving off the inevitable. It was difficult to believe that Micheal or Mercede could recover sufficiently within the foreseeable future to get up and start killing spiders, and equally difficult to believe that we could get the spiders before they got us even if they did. We couldn't keep playing forever, and the spiders certainly weren't going to go away if and when they got bored. I wondered what the galactic record for long-distance pipe-playing was, and whether the wind's ability to make better use of my body than I could would help us to break it.

Probably not, I decided. He had a lot more on his mind now than subtle tinkering with the autonomic nervous system. He probably wouldn't be able to exercise anywhere near the same fineness of control. While he was in full charge, he was probably only a shade more efficient than me. It was undoubtedly possible for me to take over his role as he was taking over mine.

But I didn't know how.

We were, implicitly, waiting for help. We had no reason to assume that any would be forthcoming in the near future. The forest people would undoubtedly return. But when?

The blackness of night arrived with its usual haste, and robbed us even of the small comfort that seeing the immobility of the enemy had afforded us. There was no light at all except for the mute red glow of the embers of our dying fire. As time went by even the redness faded away, and in the end we were left in the pitch darkness.

The song of the pipes went on and on.

I began to hate it.

Fear began to gather itself within me once again. My time sense seemed to be distorted, and logic told me that more time had passed than I had actually 'experienced'. But the time factor was nevertheless beginning to get to me. In darkness, I was subjected to a very harsh exercise in sensory deprivation. It was not so much that I could not receive any sensory input, but that I had the feeling of not being able to use my senses. I was impotent within my own body—wilfully so—and the darkness heightened that feeling. It was a situation very conducive to fear, and I couldn't help gradually descending into it as it tried to take possession of my consciousness.

I knew that the fear itself was dangerous. Fear affects not only the mind, but also the physiology. The source of fear may be located in the imagination, but the process of *feeling* scared inevitably co-opts the resources of the whole body. In the body, fear is glandular imbalance—adrenaline, vasopressor hormone imbalance, followed by pituitary imbalance. The vascular system carrying the hormones is itself the major site of reaction, but you sense it primarily in your skin. It's hot or cold, dry or sweating, stretched or heavy. Ultimate fear can black you out, or stop your heart, or...

If the fear that I was allowing to grow got too powerful, it could rob the wind of his own presence of mind. If I lost control of myself, it would have exactly the same effect as his losing control. It could kill us both. He was in the driving seat, but I knew only too well that the man in the back seat was very much a part of what went on in the car. In the Halcyon Drift, I had been forced to black out before the wind could take over, because I was consumed and paralysed by stark terror, and there was nothing to be done with the body while my imagination was feeding it fear.

Something awful could happen here, if I allowed it to.

I fought.

Side by side, the wind and I waged war on circumstance and

on our own weaknesses. If the wind gave me any active help, I was unaware of it. If I helped the wind in any way, it was not by conscious volition. But even if there was no overlap between the roles in our collective fight, the mutualism of the moment was obvious, and it made an impression on us both. It brought us far closer together than we could possibly have come by sensible and sane agreement. We were forced together, under pressure, welded to one another by desperation and the threat of bodily death.

The most logical and persistent of all my worries regarding the wind had always been the fact that bodily death was absolute only for me—he could go on to a new host. I had always feared that he might therefore be more careless of my life than I. That night, I found out that I was wrong. While attached to my mind the wind was *committed*, no less than I. He might have a cat's nine lives, but he lived them one at a time. In adapting to my brain for the purposes of living therein, he had become completely (but reversibly) humanised. He was forced by the nature of things to exactly the same level of commitment that I was. The logical, 'objective' view of his priorities was quite wrong. I discovered that while we were fighting together in the forest.

After that, it was no longer possible for me to remain apart from the wind. Inevitably, this moment was the turning point in the pathology of my own alienation.

I knew that if we were to survive, I would never be exactly the same again.

I conquered my fear.

The music played on and on, and we were steady enough and stable enough now to be sure that we could play until we dropped or until we could no longer co-ordinate the music sufficiently to paralyse the minds of the spiders.

We began to look forward to morning. It was a useful target. We knew that in the morning we would have to play ourselves through the day looking forward to evening, but that didn't matter. We had to take our markers one at a time. There was no point in contemplating the infinite or the indefinite. The problem was very definitely finite.

Night on Chao Phrya, of course, was not nearly as long as night on most of the other worlds where I had spent time during my years of wandering with Lapthorn. But it passed even more quickly than that because of the disorientation of my temporal perception. I think that on many worlds, our collective mental strength might not have sustained us through the night. Dawn, however, gave us extra strength. It was a blessing to be able to see again, even though we already knew what we were going to see. It helped our hopes to rise.

That extra burst of hope might well have saved our lives.

A few minutes after dawn, Micheal revived, and rolled lethargically away from my feet. He didn't get up. He remembered the spiders, and lay quite still, with his eyes open. I was very glad indeed to see that he was alive and well.

Mercede awoke also. Before she had a chance to open her eyes and react, Micheal had gripped her arm, and was talking to her. The words tumbled out in a fast, hissing stream. She absorbed it all, and there was not the slightest sign of panic. She did not reply. She remained passive and quiet, and the crypto-arachnids did no more than stir throughout the entire exchange.

I could not see Micheal's face once he had turned his head to speak to Mercede, so I could not savour the expression which I imagined was there. I could only guess what he had thought on awakening to find that I had played the spiders into quiescence and kept them there all night.

I think that Micheal was gathering his strength. I feel sure that as soon as he was able he would have tried to do something. What it would have been, I don't know. He knew more about the spiders than I did, and he might know something which would enable him to kill them without permitting them the freedom which had resulted from my method of attempted extermination. It is far from impossible that he would have chosen simply to take Mercede into the forest and save himself and his sister. I wouldn't have blamed him. I might well have done the same myself.

But Micheal did not need his strength.

Just as I caught the first ostentatious hint of weakness and distortion in the relentless mournful cadence which the wind was repeating over and over again, a beam of light cut a line through the dim purple morning and one of the spiders burst into flame. My eyes were dazzled, and I didn't see the rest very clearly, but I know that the beam swung, and the spiders were freed from the spell.

They moved, but they had no chance at all. The gun stopped its constant stream of fire only once, while Danel moved it past us. Then he burned the three which were at our backs.

All seven were aflame within a matter of three or four seconds. It was a beautiful piece of gunplay.

My body was suddenly my own again, and I swung around to make sure that everything was still and safe. Then I whipped around again to face Danel.

It all happened too fast. I just collapsed. As I went down, I saw someone running forward from the trees, overtaking Danel.

It was Alyne.

The panpipes dropped from my fingers and my hip landed on top of them as I folded up.

They broke.

I fainted.

CHAPTER SEVENTEEN

By THE TIME I AWOKE, we had gained a great deal more company. There were people everywhere. Forest people, and others.

I half-expected to find a ring of concerned faces peering at me, but my fragmentary dreams of people and spiders and panpipes had taken time away from me, and I did not immediately realise that my faint had released me into a deep sleep and that a good many hours had passed. It was almost night now.

I was propped against a pile of rock, and my head was pillowed on a folded garment of some kind. Micheal and Mercede were laid out to my right, both sleeping, wrapped in blankets and apparently comfortable. Linda and Danel sat between them, watching over them.

Watching over me were Eve Lapthorn and the girl I had met in the hills near Corinth.

'Hi,' said Eve quietly, as I sat up and stretched to take away some of the stiffness. I felt pained.

'Welcome to the party,' I said. 'I see you brought home the baby. Congratulations.'

'Not quite,' she said. 'The baby brought me. I was lost in the forest.'

'Surprise surprise,' I said, never having doubted for a moment that that was the way it had happened.

I looked at Alyne. Her knees were tucked up under her chin, and she was curling her toes reflectively. Her toes, like her fingers, were remarkably susceptible to curling.

'Suddenly,' I said, not particularly to the girl or to Eve, 'everything is coming up roses. Not only the US Cavalry, but also the golden girl. I haven't had so much luck in one day since....'

And I stopped, because I couldn't think of an example. I could tell by the way that my wit ran away with my tongue that I was all right.

Everything was all right, it seemed. The forest people had tidied up completely.

'Wow,' I said.

Eve was looking at me with a mixture of puzzlement and amusement. The girl's expression was quite unreadable.

'Is Micheal okay?' I asked. ' Eve nodded.

Danel left his brother and sister to come over and look at me. I raised my hand in a mock salute which I meant quite seriously.

'Thanks a lot,' I said. 'That was first-class shooting.'

He hesitated, and then he nodded, but I think he was replying to the salute rather than to what I'd said.

'You sure you're all right?' asked Eve.

'Sure,' I said. 'But hungry. Very, very hungry. Also in need of a shot, but shots we don't have. I'll settle for the food.'

'It'll only take a minute,' she said, and she got up and went away. She turned round a few paces away and said: 'There's someone who wants to talk to us.'

'Not Max?'

'The kidnapper,' she said.

'Bully for her,' I replied. 'We'll fit her in after the main course and not a minute before.' Actually, I was very keen for a chance to talk to someone who could presumably explain this whole sad and sorry mess, but protocol has to be observed.

I returned my attention to Danel and the girl. I knew that neither of them would understand a word I said, so I didn't bother talking. The three of us just sat quietly together until Eve came back with some food. Nothing happened, but I don't think the time was wasted. It was something that we sat *together*. Danel couldn't thank me for saving his brother and sister any more than I could thank him for saving me. But I think we conveyed what was necessary without a word or a gesture.

The woman appeared immediately after the main course, just as I'd said. Danel left then, but the girl stayed. She didn't show any reaction at all to the woman. There was no evidence of any hostility between them. So where did that leave the kidnap theory?

'Your name is Grainger,' she said.

'That's right.'

'You're here on behalf of Titus Charlot?'

'She is,' I said, pointing to Eve. 'I only work here.'

The woman didn't appreciate the flippancy. She could hardly be expected to. After all, she was on the brink of big trouble.

'It's all right,' I said. 'I don't think there's any necessity to take you back if you don't want to go. The girl will have to come, though. Just explain it all to us, please. Not just for Charlot—for me.'

'What do you know about the colony?' she asked

'Not a lot,' I told her.

'Alyne knows you.'

'We met. I gave her a ride once. She seemed to be in a bit of trouble. I'm afraid I didn't really succeed in getting her out of it. The cops grabbed her.'

She looked at me, coolly and closely. I think my attitude was putting her off. She obviously knew a lot more about this than I did, but she didn't know anything about me.

'Look,' I said. 'I think we can short-circuit this fencing process. I'll tell you where I stand. If Eve wants to tell you something different, that's up to her. I work for Charlot. I've nothing to do with the colony and I know nothing about it. Just for the record, I don't like Charlot or his methods, but that's irrelevant. He told me that you'd bribed Tyler and kidnapped the girl. He didn't know why. He told me you weren't the girl's mother, and that seemed to put a little meaning into the kidnap charge. I was sent to bring the girl back, and that's what I intend to do unless you can give me some very strong reasons which she's willing to back up. I have no immediate intention of returning you for trial or whatever else Charlot might have in mind. You can stay, provided that you can sort out things with the *Zodiac* people. Okay?'

'Alyne can go back,' she said calmly. 'We're finished here. I didn't take her against her will. She knew what I was doing and why.'

'Did she understand?' asked Eve. 'She's only a child.'

'She couldn't possibly understand the significance of what I was doing,' the woman admitted. 'She is only a child. But she is also an Indris. She knew.'

'Fine,' I said. 'We'll accept that. Tell us the whole story.'

And she did, and this was it:

'All of the people who were recruited for the colony were volunteers from the territory which was occupied by the *Zodiac* people. The New Alexandrians wanted to know what we could show them, and we wanted to know what they could show us. I think most of us intended to come back, but that intention was gradually lost over the years except in one or two of us. There was no point in coming back unless we had something to show for the years we spent on New Alexandria. But we had very little. We learned hardly anything from the New Alexandrians that we had not already learned from the people of the *Zodiac*. All that we learned was that you cannot understand us.

'We are alien to you, but you are not alien to us. We do not have any concept of alienness. We do not have any concept of separateness from anyone or anything. We do not think in terms of selves.

'We have adaptable minds. Some of us have absorbed human-ness from you. We cannot become human to our own minds or to each other, but we can become almost human to you. You can be sure of us. You can give us motives. You can give us selves. You can give us everything that you have, and it makes sense to you. But you cannot understand what we are in our language and in each other. You cannot communicate with us as what we are. You can only communicate with the humanness that you give us. You cannot understand our language. You cannot understand what our language *is*, because it is not the same as yours.

'Some of us, both here on Chao Phrya and in the Anacaon colony, cannot learn your language because they do not want to accept the humanness that they would have to take into themselves in order to do so. It is the only way for us to learn. The languages do not translate. The other modes of communication you do not have.

'In the Anacaon language, there is no deception. There is no misunderstanding. There is no philosophy. There is no ontology.

'The colony on New Alexandria is a glass cage. We watch and we are watched. The profit of that watching is very little. This makes your people watch all the harder. Titus Charlot could never be content with a lack of understanding, and he could never accept the possibility that he could never understand. He experimented. We co-operated, of course.

'The New Alexandrians did not like us. They tried, but they failed. I think it is because we were an offence against their vanity. We *seemed* to be so much nearer communication than they. We could speak your language, but your people could not speak ours. We could interpret motives in your language. We could interpret philosophical concepts in your language. Your people could not understand that this was a feature of our adaptability. It was not of our *selves*, because we had no selves except for the ones which your people had given us. Not even Titus Charlot, who is a brilliant man, could accept that we could use your channels of communication only in a passive way. His point of view did not permit him to consider the communication problem in the right way. He has no conception of what it is like not to be apart. He cannot see that only we are different from him. He is not different from us.

'Alyne was the experiment that Titus Charlot wanted to try in order that he might bridge the gap which he saw between us. Alyne was conceived in a machine. She grew inside the machine, and the machine tampered with the development of the embryo. It did not replace or alter any of the genes, but it reorganised the filters in the hierarchical system which governed the expression of the genes. Charlot told us that the purpose was to make an intimate study of Anacaon developmental biology. Perhaps this was true. But he knew what we could tell him about the Indris. He could hardly have created an Indris by accident. I do not know how many other embryos there were. Alyne was the only one who was born from the machine. She was given to a pair of Anacaon parents. I was not one of them.

'I think that Charlot's intention all along was to recreate our parent race. He had made a guess which he was trying to confirm. He built a conceptual equation in which to be without a self was to be without a soul. He believed that the Indris did have selves. He believed that the fact that we had not indicated that they were not only our ancestors, but our creators and designers.

'He thought that we were androids, created by tissue-culture and shaped by manipulation of genetic expressivity and modulation. He thought that he could reverse the process. The experiment was a success.

'Alyne is an Indris. She speaks a language like ours, but she speaks it in your way. Her language can be translated, and therefore Titus Charlot thinks she is the link which he needed and the key to the Anacaon problem. I think he is right. Alyne has our channels of communication but your way of communicating. She can teach you. But she can also teach us. The people of the *Zodiac* have given us humanness. I think that we also need to have Indrisness. Perhaps I would not think this way if I had not already been given humanity. I think not. Titus Charlot had given himself access to our false gods. I wanted us to have it as well. Most of all, I wanted the forest people to have it. The people at the colony have all been given humanness. Because of that, we felt confused. We were unsure of our communication with Alyne. We had to bring her back here, to people who knew nothing about humanness. We had to know whether she really could communicate the being of the Indris, along our channels, and not merely through our humanness. It is almost impossible to explain, because you have no idea of the sort of communication I am talking about. It is not communication which involves two people or two hundred. It is communication involving words and music and other things, all in themselves and not as coded symbols.

'It had to be now. It had to be before Charlot started to talk to her himself. It had to be before she was old enough to become humanised. Charlot said: "Not now—later." He did not understand. I brought her back. I had to. She had to sing to the forest people. She had to speak to them. She had to be part of Chao Phrya, and the universe. She had to be home in order to be at all. Before Titus Charlot made her into a human being. I wanted to give the Indris back to my people.

'You know what the Indris made my people into, and I think you know why. That, you should be able to understand. The Indris are within your mental reach, even if the Anacaona are not. You can see what the Indris were trying to do. You know why they made us selfless. You know why they made us tractable. You know why they made us truthful. You know why they made us to be a part of the world they shaped us for, and a part of the existence that we were sharing with them. You do understand *that*, at least, don't you?'

I understood *that* all right.

It was something to do with paradise. They had called themselves gods. Someday, this whole story could be about us. Once we had finished our games of conquest, our games of empire and our games of shaping, we would try our hands at the game of god. It was inevitable. We had a name for the syndrome even now.

Promised Land.

CHAPTER EIGHTEEN

I COULD SENSE A LOT of the importance which Charlot ascribed to this project. The Indris were a starfaring race that we had lost. Not dead, in all likelihood, but not the lords of space and time despite the head start they had on us and on the Gallacellans and on the Khor-monsa. That was a first-magnitude problem in itself. But there was something even worse than that. If we were to do what the Indris had so patently failed to do—play *all* of our games and win the lot—then we would have to know the answer to one vital question:

Why couldn't the Indris understand their own creations? Their androids, their robots, their clay people?

That they couldn't was implicit in the whole story that the woman told us. Out of their own flesh and blood they had created a people that they couldn't understand. It was not a matter of the Anacaona being more 'advanced' or more 'highly evolved'. That was a simplistic view. They were just different. What did it signify that complete alienness was so close at hand to these people? Was alienness that much closer to us than we had ever suspected?

I didn't understand the Anacaona. I couldn't make head nor tail of their thinking processes. The woman's explanation, inevitably, was just so much doubletalk. Charlot would see it the same way. But I was content not to understand. I was content to think in terms of Danel having shot the spiders and saved my life, of Micheal getting sick and playing the pipes, and being unable to play the pipes, and my saving all our lives. That was what the golden people meant to me.

But Titus Charlot couldn't think in anything like those terms.

If you're going to play the game of god you can't live on the plane of things happening to you and what those things do to you.

If the Anacaon woman was right in saying that Charlot couldn't ever understand (and I didn't necessarily accept that she *was* right), then Charlot's game was a loser. His ambitions of providing the foundation stone for a monadistic intellectual edifice encompassing the galaxy and all its mysteries were just so much waste. No wonder he prized Alyne pretty highly. No wonder he hadn't wanted to let her out of his sight for even a moment. No wonder the Anacaona had been forced to resort to kidnap. Not just one, but all of them. It *had* to be all of them, or they would never have found the money to bribe Tyler and the captain of the *White Fire*. And, perhaps least of all, no wonder that Tyler and his friend had been so mad keen to recover the girl from her innocent little walk, and why the cops had been called out with such desperate alacrity.

Alyne was worth her weight in Titus Charlot's vanity. And there was nothing in the universe that Titus Charlot measured more highly than that.

I felt sure that the woman was telling the truth. I also felt sure that she had given us as full an account of her reasons as she could. If there were any lies therein, or misunderstandings, or misinterpretations, it was the language that lied and not her.

Eve found it all impossible to accept. She didn't see how it was possible that the Indris—or anyone else—could create something that was beyond their understanding. The woman only offered one extra argument.

She said: 'Can you humans understand your children? *Before* you have managed to turn them into human beings?'

I thought it was a good point.

We set off for home the next morning. Micheal and Mercede had not recovered enough to make the journey back with us, and Danel stayed with them in the forest. We were escorted back to the edge of the forest by half a dozen of the forest people. The woman did not come with us even this far. She stayed too.

Max was not with us. We later learned that he had contrived to remain unfound by the Anacaona, and had eventually made his own way back out of the jungle. On arriving back at the town we had left, he had tried to give the supply base the sad news of our death. They corrected him mildly, and explained that they had been dropping food to us for three days.

He waited for us to arrive. He beat us by just six hours. He didn't seem overly pleased to see us.

In view of his unfortunate attitude to the way the thing had turned out, I was forced to ask Linda to carry out two small commissions for me.

I had not been able to talk to Micheal again before we left, and I had not had the opportunity to express my regrets concerning the loss of his pipes. I asked Linda to secure him a new set on my behalf, and give them to him with my apologies for my carelessness.

I had a long talk with Linda about the Anacaona. I tried to tell her all the things which I felt she should have been able to tell me before we even started on the expedition. I told her about the direct communication between mind and environment which they apparently possessed. I stressed the importance of their language and their music in binding them to each other and to the world around them. I explained the kidnapping by telling her that the woman had been trying to restore to the forest people the gods which had declared themselves to be false and then had abandoned their children so many years ago. The parents had needed to understand, and did not. The children did not need to understand—they just needed to *be*, and the girl could help them to be.

That's where I lost her. She accepted my interpretation of the legend of the Indris. Despite her commitment to the Promised Land she couldn't refuse to acknowledge that there had been others here before, and that for them also it had been a Promised Land and a chance to regain paradise. But the story never really cast any shadows on her prejudices. For her, the sets of facts could exist side by side with her fixed beliefs.

She was sincere. She was a nice person. I liked her. But I couldn't help myself feeling just a little sorry for her. It's arrogant, I know, but that's what I felt. To me she seemed basically empty. The Anacaona had surrendered their self to their space. Linda had never managed to connect hers, except by the belief in the Promised Land. She and the people she purported to study were polar opposites.

It was not for me to offer her advice or try to provoke a change in her. I told her what I knew, and I ladled sarcasm onto some of her reactions. She didn't take offence, because she knew no malice was intended. She didn't take any notice either.

We left Linda in the town, and only Max was with us when we set off on our long journey back to the port..

It was not good to see the sun again. Any psychological fillip was easily outweighed by the physical discomfort. I had to wear dark glasses all day every day for all the time it took to get ourselves and Alyne bank to the *Hooded Swan*. The same applied to Max and Eve. As it was not high summer we must have looked like a soap-opera version of the Mafia.

'It's too bad you've had so much trouble here,' said Max at one point, while we were waiting for the train after relinquishing the hovercraft. 'It's really a very fine world. We're really making something of it, as you can see. It's a pity you can't give us better publicity out there.'

'I don't think so,' I told him. 'The last thing you people need is publicity. We haven't got a distorted view of this world. You have. It's us that have got the cosmic perspective, remember.'

'By that logic,' he said, 'all groundhogs would have a distorted impression of their own environment.'

'All people,' I corrected him. He didn't even begin to see what I was getting at.

'Well,' he said, 'I guess it isn't important what you think anyhow. When all is said and done, you're not very important yourselves.'

'That's me,' I said happily. 'Absolutely unimportant. What I think doesn't matter a damn to anyone but me. Who'd be any other way, if they stopped to think?'

He didn't appreciate that either. Nor did Eve. She still had a lot of maturity to beat into her skull. She cared too much about the wrong things.

By the time we got back to the port, Alyne could speak a good fifty words of English. Mostly, I hasten to add, courtesy of Eve's helpful nature. Eve didn't believe in silences. She thought they only existed to be broken. The girl was most receptive to conversation, and Eve found her pleasant company, if only because she wasn't sarcastic. It wasn't enough for Eve that the kid could smile and make the occasional friendly gesture. Eve took it as her duty to teach the girl our names and allow her to tell us how happy she was, and how fast the train was going.

I found the process somewhat sickening and grotesque. I felt no particular need to express myself to the girl, but if I had I would have found some means by which I could communicate at a level which enabled us to mean something when we said something. Words for the sake of making a noise seemed to me to be an insult to Eve, to Alyne and to intelligence in general. But I didn't say anything. No doubt Titus Charlot would thank Eve for helping him get started with Alyne. Either that or he would half-kill her for interfering with his experiment.

When we eventually arrived back at the *Swan* we were not rapturously received. Charlot had been kicking his heels for far too long, and everyone had been consistently rude to him. Although he had no doubt been delighted when he heard that the girl had been recovered, several days had passed since then and his elation had long ago been swamped by impatience.

I had no wish to talk to him about the girl. I knew it could only lead to a very long and very unprofitable discussion of all sorts of principles which I was quite happy to live with instead of arguing about. I left it to Eve to relay what she could of the woman's account. It was her job—she had been in charge of the expedition. I was only the hired help. I wasn't in the least interested in holding hours of intellectual discussion with Charlot about abstruse points in the woman's story. I didn't envy Eve the task of telling him the whole story, and I had no intention of involving myself. I was quite content to pilot the *Swan* back to Corinth and consign the whole affair to the depths of memory.

After I had slept off all the worst effects of the journey, with the aid of some proper medicine.

When I finally did lift the bird to put a full stop to the whole story, I reflected that I was even gladder to get away from Chao Phrya than I had been to get away from Rhapsody. I knew that in my own inimitable fashion I remained completely untouched by the world, and that the only thing I carried away from the world was a small parcel in my pocket, which was the result of the second commission which I had asked Linda to carry out for me before we left the edge of the forest.

But significant things had happened during the Chao Phrya mission. I was more firmly bonded to the wind. We were, at last, twin souls. I had needed the wind in the Halcyon Drift, and possibly in the warren on Rhapsody, but that need had been of a different quality. Ever since the moment when I had picked up Micheal's pipes, and until death us did part, I would never stop needing him.

While I relaxed in the cradle *en route* for New Alexandria, I reminded myself of my—our—continuing obligation to Charlot. I counted off the days that had gone by while we were down on the planet. It didn't seem so many, once it was translated back from local to standard. My contract had a long way to run.

What next? I wondered.

Does it matter? asked the wind.

Not a lot, I conceded. The important thing is endurance. The first year and a half is the worst. The last six months will just fly.

I was being mildly sarcastic.

He laughed.

It came as something of a surprise.

It's a hard life, I commented.

It could be worse, he said.

Yeah, I said. It could be raining.

CHAPTER NINETEEN

THE STORY HAS A POSTSCRIPT.

I met the ex-bodyguard in a bar the night after we landed on New Alexandria. We just sort of bumped into one another. He'd been reassigned while Charlot was out of local police jurisdiction, and he didn't have the same opportunities for hanging around any more. But he had come looking for me as soon as he could. He was out of uniform and looked almost human.

'You brought her back, then?' he said.

'Sure did,' I replied.

'And?'

'You owe me a drink.'

'Can you prove that in a court of law?'

'No. You'll have to take my word for it.'

He curled his lip, then turned away and ordered the drinks. I drank it slowly. I enjoyed it. I always enjoy winning bets.

'Ever been in space?' I asked him.

'No.'

'Strictly a groundhog, then?'

'You could put it that way.'

'I just did. You know, the trouble with people who stay grounded all their lives is that they lack the cosmic perspective. You feel particularly attached to the holy soil of New Alexandria?'

'In a way,' Denton replied. 'Not passionately.'

'It serves its purpose, hey?'

'It always looked okay to me.'

'You've never felt the wanderlust?'

'A bit. Nothing I couldn't handle.'

I smiled at his choice of phrase. 'Did you ever feel a driving need to *understand* the workings of the universe?' I asked him. 'Would you feel yourself to be incomplete or unfulfilled if you had to leave stones unturned in your search for the meaning of life?'

'I don't think so.'

'No unconquerable lust for understanding?'

'No.'

He was smiling, waiting for me to tell him what the hell I was talking about.

'That's good,' I said. 'Me neither. I like it. But I do like to *know*, don't you? I do like looking under stones. Do you suppose it might become pathological? Or do you think the whole concept of the Library is curiosity gone insane?'

He was bewildered by the swift change of emphasis.

'I don't know,' he said.

'Me neither,' I said again. 'May I buy you a drink?'

'I thought it was your turn to say "I told you so".'

'It is,' I said. 'I told you so. Now I'm offering to buy you a drink out of the kindness of my heart.'

'Thank you,' he said. I bought another round.

'Aren't you going to tell me the whole story?' he asked.

'I guess so,' I said. 'But we'd better get some more drinks in. They'll make it seem that much less boring.'

While I was speaking, I fished the little parcel out of my pocket. I unwrapped it, stood the contents on end on the bar, and looked at them pensively.

'What's that?' asked Denton.

'It's a present. For Titus Charlot. I haven't given them to him yet. They're to help him to his quest for understanding. They're a research tool of great value.'

'Yes,' said the cop. 'But what is it?'

'It's a set of panpipes,' I said.

ABOUT THE AUTHOR

Brian Stableford was born in Yorkshire in 1948. He taught at the University of Reading for several years, but is now a full-time writer. He has written many science-fiction and fantasy novels, including *The Empire of Fear*, *The Werewolves of London*, *Year Zero*, *The Curse of the Coral Bride*, *The Stones of Camelot*, and *Prelude to Eternity*. Collections of his short stories include a long series of *Tales of the Biotech Revolution*, and such idiosyncratic items as *Sheena and Other Gothic Tales* and *The Innsmouth Heritage and Other Sequels*. He has written numerous nonfiction books, including *Scientific Romance in Britain, 1890-1950*; *Glorious Perversity: The Decline and Fall of Literary Decadence*; *Science Fact and Science Fiction: An Encyclopedia*; and *The Devil's Party: A Brief History of Satanic Abuse*. He has contributed hundreds of biographical and critical articles to reference books, and has also translated numerous novels from the French language, including books by Paul Féval, Albert Robida, Maurice Renard, and J. H. Rosny the Elder.

www.ingramcontent.com/pod-product-compliance
Lightning Source LLC
Chambersburg PA
CBHW050749250626
47155CB00005B/1985